Guardian of the Shadow Warrior

A Novel

by

D. S. Cuellar

壱

弐

Guardian of the Shadow Warrior

Visit us on Facebook at

Guardian of the Red Butterfly

Cover Design by Roslyn McFarland

Other novels:

Guardian of the Red Butterfly

Guardian of the Monarch Moon

Dead to Rights

参

Special Thanks to:

Editor:

Pauline Suite

Technical Support:

Ryan Wintersteen

A special thanks to

David Morrell

for his encouragement and correspondence.

四

GUARDIAN OF THE SHADOW WARRIOR

CHAPTER 1

He was a husband and a father. He had everything. He was the most powerful man in the world and was just brought to his knees.

Spencer Dalton, The President of the United States, was aboard Air Force One that was parked on the tarmac at the private terminals of Andrews Air Force Base in Maryland, Virginia.

The area had been secured and agents in tactical gear had their positions covered from nearby surroundings, from the rooftops to the ground. Two of his secret service agents, Hauge and Segar, were at their post at the bottom of stairs.

Inside, Pres. Dalton, was in his private office sitting at his desk. A battered and bruised Kyle Morrell was sitting across from him.

"Was she worth it?" Dalton asked.

Dalton took a sip of his drink.

Kyle didn't hesitate. "She was worth it."

Dalton took another sip of his drink and it went down hard. "Everything has a cost."

Kyle's non-response spoke volumes and after everything he had been through in the last few days, Kyle still had enough anger in him to want to finish this once and for all. Kyle's hands were gripping the end of the chair's leather arms so tight that his fingertips were turning white.

There was a soft knock just outside the door frame. Oksana entered, and she too had a few scratches and bruises. She was wearing a new commemorative T-shirt that still had the fold creases. It was adorned with a large AF-1 logo on it and was one size too big for her. She took up the slack by tying a knot in the front of it at the waist. Her hair was a bit matted and dirty. Kyle stood as best he could over his aching knee and started to walk with Oksana down the center corridor that led to the front exit of the plane.

The First Lady, Jillian Dalton, approached the office area and met them at the door wearing a blue dress.

Jillian took Oksana by the hand. "Let me walk you out, Oksana. I want to thank you for everything. After all, if it wasn't for you, I would not be here."

Jillian and Oksana walked heading to the forward exit that was located just behind just the cockpit of the Boeing 747.

Dalton spoke up getting Kyle's attention. "Kyle, if you had the chance, would you do it all over again knowing what you know now?"

Kyle stopped. "In a heartbeat." Kyle looked down through the four-thousand square foot plane and watched as Jillian and Oksana walked off the plane and out into the bright sunlight, as they left Air Force One.

*****

The Oregon night sky at Portland International Airport was clear.

Air Force One was parked on the private part of the tarmac just North-East of the main terminal. Secret Service agents had their assigned positions and agents, Hauge and Segar, were at their post at the bottom of the stairs.

Jillian and Oksana were at the top of the portable stairs that were pressed up to the side of the plane. The First Lady was wearing a white summer dress that her husband, Spencer, The President, liked to see her in. She had Oksana by the hand as they walked down the steps hand in hand.

Oksana looked happy and refreshed as her hair twisted in the warm summer wind. She was wearing a red button-down shirt, worn blue jeans, and white Converse sneakers. They walked across the tarmac toward the main building that made up the airport's interior followed by the First Lady's two Secret Service agents, Weller and Lynch.

Jillian was just as anxious as Oksana to get off the plane and stretch her legs. She didn't mind the five-hour flight from Washington D.C. to Portland as she had a scheduled event the next day. She liked the idea that her human rights seminar would be taking place on Independence Day. It had a ring to it.

"Oksana, are you ready to see the fireworks tomorrow night? I heard that this is one of the best places in the area to see them. It's my understanding the top-level of the parking garage is the best place to observe the firework show from."

"Yes. Will you be back in time to see them with me?"

"I wouldn't miss it. Would you like to go inside to the food court and get an ice cream?"

"Can I get it on a waffle cone?"

"Sure, and I know just the place."

*****

Inside Air Force One, Pres. Dalton was in his private suite. He stood at the minibar pouring himself a drink and took a seat at his desk. Kyle Morrell looked refreshed and ready to go and was patiently sitting across from him. He was admiring the plush leather staff chair he sat in. He was thinking how great it would be to have this for the driver's seat in his car.

"Before you say anything, I cleared it with my doctor. I can have one drink a day."

"I can't believe your doctor allowed you to follow the First Lady to Portland."

"It took a little negotiating, but I insisted I wanted to show my support for Jillian's fundraiser."

"So, everything is going well?"

"Yes. Thanks to Oksana and the bone marrow transplant, everything seems to be on track to a full recovery. She's a great kid. You and Aiko have done a fine job with her."

"I have to give Aiko most of the credit." He reached over to Aiko, sitting in the chair next to him, and took her hand.

Kyle smiled as he looked at Aiko. "I think all of the training these two have been doing together has helped her with her recovery as well."

Pres. Dalton raised his glass. "I understand congratulations are in order. Do you know if Oksana is going to have a little brother or a little sister?"

"Thank you, Mr. President," Kyle replied. "I am afraid it is a little too early to tell."

Aiko was surprised he knew. She looked at Kyle and squeezed his hand. Kyle apologized for having already told the president by rubbing his thumb across the back of her hand.

Dalton sensed she wasn't quite ready to talk about it, so he settled back into his chair, thought it was time to get into the specifics of the meeting, and pulled out two files from the top desk drawer. He laid them on his desk in front of Kyle and Aiko.

Dalton's voice had changed from a family man to presidential. "With everything that is going on, are you two sure you're ready to start looking for your team to lead up this redemption mission?"

Aiko squeezed Kyle's hand to let Kyle know she was in agreement. "Yes, sir. I've talked with your wife. Tracking down these missing girls is going to be a great start to showing the First Lady's concerns for all of the human trafficking that goes on around the world."

"Yes, and in fact Aiko, that is what drew me to her. Her love for making a change for all the young people who have been exploited around the world. She told me she wanted to give them back their hope."

"Yes, she is a wonderful lady," Aiko said.

Dalton felt confident. "Well then, let's not waste any more time." Dalton handed Kyle one of the files, a dossier. "I've already got your first member. His name is John Casey. He has special ops training and will help you run point and be your financier. Whatever you need, he'll make it happen."

Kyle knew this was the right thing for him and Aiko, to help them get a fresh start in this, their new roles as a team. "Thank you, Sir."

Dalton reiterated, "Now remember, this project is on a need to know basis. We can't have any leaks getting out and compromising any of our team members while on a recovery mission. These first few targets are powerful men and we need to go by the numbers on this one. If we can justify the results, we can extend the budget."

Dalton opened the second file and showed Kyle and Aiko its contents. The first thing Kyle saw was a ledger with a $5 million budget.

CHAPTER 2

Inside Portland international Airport the First Lady and Oksana were walking with their single scoop chocolate ice cream cones, followed by Secret Service agent Weller as agent Segar was a few yards away, still paying for the ice cream.

Oksana put the palm of her hand to her forehead. She sensed a brain freeze coming on and had to slow down. "I love chocolate. It's the best."

Jillian licked a drip of ice cream that was starting to run down the back of one of her fingers. "I agree."

As Jillian and Oksana walked down the middle of the breezeway, a few onlookers realized it was the First Lady. Agent Weller saw them too and with just a look, kept the onlookers a bay.

"I'm glad my event schedule on human trafficking brought me back through Portland. It's been two months since the bone marrow transplant and I wanted to thank you personally for what you did."

"He is my father."

"Yes, he is. Have you decided what you're going to call him?"

"I know he's the president and all, but I can't keep calling him that."

"No, that might be a little much."

"My father turned out not to be my father and I'm closer to Kyle than anyone else. Dad seems to be not quite right. Can I just call him, D?"

"I think he'd like that."

The breezeway began to fill quickly with band members of all kinds heading in both directions.

Oksana got bumped and lost her ice cream. "Hey!" She knelt to pick up what was left of her ice cream and as she did, she noticed the First Lady's feet being dragged away. Looking up, Oksana saw two men in black, each had Jillian's arms around their shoulders pulling her away. The crowd was becoming overwhelming and Jillian and Oksana were separated.

"Jillian!"

Oksana stood and went to follow but was blocked and pushed back by two women who were also dressed in a dark Goth-like attire. By the time she worked her way through the crowd, she had lost sight of the First Lady.

There was no response from the First Lady. Both Secret Service agents reached Oksana at the same time. Both men quickly surmised the First Lady was gone. Agent Weller started to take a step and then saw just a few feet away, was a single scoop of chocolate ice cream that had slid about a foot across the tile floor. It left a trail of melted chocolate leading away. Just beyond that was a bit of the sugar cone, and beyond that more of the sugar cone. Had the First Lady left a trail in the direction she was taken?

Weller went to his COM's, "We've lost majestic! Send back up!"

More band members from various bands hauling their equipment filled the breezeway making it harder for the Secret Service agents to get a good look in any direction.

*****

The two Secret Service agents, Hauge and Segar, who were on duty at the bottom of the portable stairs, ran in the direction of the airport lobby as two more Secret Service agents came down the stairs and took up their new positions at the bottom.

Inside Air Force One, Dalton was on the phone. "Thank you, Captain."

Dalton hung up the phone.

"Is it true?" Kyle asked. "Someone has kidnapped the First Lady? Do they have Oksana?"

Pres. Dalton regained his focus. "That was head of security here at PDX. Yes, it appears that someone or some group has kidnapped Jillian. They're going over all the security cameras as we speak."

"And Oksana?" Aiko asked.

Dalton replied, "My men have her in the main lobby. She's okay."

*****

The automatic doors opened and allowed Kyle and Aiko to enter the main breezeway of the airport from the North end of the complex. Aiko followed Kyle's lead as they ran through the airport. As they reached the busy lobby, they found agents Weller and Lynch, but no Oksana.

Kyle looked around confused. "Where's the girl? Where is Oksana?"

Agent Weller was still scanning the crowd. "Right after we reported in, she said she saw the First Lady and took off running."

Aiko stepped in. "Which way did she go?"

Agent Weller pointed down the breezeway. "That way, South."

Immediately Kyle and Aiko took off running South through the lobby, pushing their way through the hustle and bustle of the large crowd.

At the South end of the breezeway, a group of six band members all dressed in various combinations of black, were huddling in a tight circle as two of the larger men were helping what appeared to be a drunken, barefoot, female bandmember walk. The woman they were helping was the First Lady. She had been drugged.

They had wrapped her lower body in a black blanket, so it looked like she was wearing a long skirt. They also slipped her into a black leather jacket and black wig highlighted with green and blue one-inch stripes.

The group comprised of men and women were dressed up as goth bandmates burst through a set of double doors that led outside to an open holding area.

Back inside the lobby, Oksana had stopped and was scanning in all directions. She stood on the seat of a bench for a better view over the crowd. She then stepped up on the armrest of the bench to get even higher. She looked in the direction she last saw Jillian and got a short look at a man as he tossed a pair of high-end white lady's dress shoes into a garbage can before following his bandmates out the set of double doors. As the man went out the door he looked back. Just as the doors closed, Oksana could see on the man's neck a large tattoo of a cross with what looked like a set of rosary beads made of white pearls wrapped around it.

Oksana jumped off the bench and stumbled into the crowd knocking over a piece of luggage a man was pulling behind him.

Oksana didn't even look back but yelled, "Sorry." She continued working her way through the crowd as she ran toward the doors. In the middle of the lobby, Kyle and Aiko were looking through the crowd. They saw Oksana jump off the bench and run in the opposite direction. They both took off running after her having to fight their way through the mass of people and bags.

Oksana stopped at the garbage can, reached in, and pulled out the First Lady's white dress shoes. Kyle and Aiko came running up behind her.

"Oksana are you alright?" Kyle asked.

"Yes. I saw the men who took her, and they just went out this door. One of them had a cross tattoo on the left side of his neck."

Kyle pushed open the doors. As he emerged he was followed by Aiko and Oksana. They saw that the busy crowd outside was worse than inside. Kyle got the feeling that five planes carrying bands from L.A. and San Francisco must have landed within the last 15 minutes of each other. The loading area was crowded with at least 100 people and eighty percent of those, band members.

Kyle had to reign in his emotions and be a cop, and not act like a panicked father. "There's got to be at least a dozen bands here all trying to load at once."

Kyle, Aiko, and Oksana started to quickly work their way through the groups looking for any sign of the First Lady. Off to one side were three 10 x 10 portable canopies that appeared to be temporary holding stages stuffed with band equipment.

The group that carried the First Lady headed into the second tent. Inside the center area of the tent, two men had cleared a space and were waiting. They had walled off two sides of the area with large band equipment cases to hide behind as cover.

One band member, Niles, opened a large travel case used to carry an upright bass that was covered in destination stickers. A few of the stickers had holes in them and were doubling as camouflage over a set of half inch drill holes used as air vents. The two men had already removed the upright bass from its case and had it set aside. The space inside the case would be a tight fit so the bandmates removed the black jacket, wig, and blanket before they loaded the First Lady into the case.

Once they had her stuffed inside, they latched the case and got it upright so it could roll on its wheels. Niles was unaware that a three-inch piece of Jillian's dress was sticking out of the case.

Outside the tent, the band members began to head out for the curb, each of them with their hands full of gear. Niles let two of the guys go ahead of him to clear the way as two others watched for anyone following or taking too much of an interest in them. Once Niles reached the curb, he signaled to a nearby van to pull up to the curb, but the area was packed, and they needed to wait a minute for it to clear. In the meantime, they awkwardly laid the case down at the curb.

Nearby, Kyle, Aiko, and Oksana were searching frantically. Kyle investigated all three tents and the now empty holding area in the middle and saw an upright bass without the case. Kyle ran out from under the tent and joined Aiko and Oksana. "I just saw a band with a large brown upright case. It is about six feet tall on wheels and has a bunch of stickers on it."

Aiko asked, "You think they have Jillian?"

"It is certainly large enough."

Kyle looked all around and saw no signs of the band or the upright case. Kyle, Aiko, and Oksana separated to cover more ground.

On the street, the curb area finally cleared, and a tour van pulled up. Niles knelt to pick up the case and he saw a white piece of dress that was sticking out. He took a quick glance around before taking the chance to open the case ever so slightly and tucked the dress back in.

At that moment, Oksana happened to be a few yards behind him in his blind spot and had a clear view to see enough of Jillian's dress inside the case to know they had the First Lady. Oksana quickly looked around to find Kyle or Aiko but at that moment, she could not take the chance to go find them over losing sight of the case holding the First Lady.

*****

Agents Weller and Segar along with an airport officer approached Kyle. Aiko had circled back and joined them.

Kyle got the officer's attention. "Call whoever you have to and get them to check the security footage going back five minutes ago and see if they can see a band taking a large upright bass through here. It's a six-foot brown case, well worn, and covered with stickers."

The officer got on his radio and called command.

Agent Lynch turned to Kyle, "What do you have?"

"I'm not sure. We were out the door right behind them and ran into this mess. I did see a band rolling a large upright case through here about five minutes ago and then found the instrument itself in one of the tents."

"So, you think they have the First Lady in the case? Where did you see the case last?" The agent asked.

"Headed toward a group of vans parked over at the curb."

The airport officer interrupted Kyle, "They saw a large upright case being loaded into a white tour van. As the van was pulling away, they saw a young girl hop onto the ladder on the back door and climb up onto the luggage rack on top of the van."

Kyle looked around and saw Oksana was nowhere in sight.

CHAPTER 3

Oksana was riding on top of the tour van with the luggage and was holding on for dear life. She pushed the larger pieces of luggage to the side and turned two of the soft pieces on their sides and got on top of them and held on.

Inside, the band members pulled off their long wigs and quickly changed out of their clothes from band members to construction workers. Niles opened a large garbage bag and all the clothes, wigs, and band paraphernalia were stuffed in.

A couple of band members squirted some rubbing alcohol onto some rags and started rubbing off their fake tattoos then tossed the rags into the garbage bag as well.

Oksana had just wedged herself in tightly with the luggage when suddenly, the van turned onto a side street and was headed toward a parking garage located near a construction site.

The tour van pulled into the construction storage lot. As the van passed by a large flatbed truck, the driver moved the flatbed forward to block the entrance to the lot.

The van circled, backed in, and pulled up under a large canopy and stopped next to a man dressed as a construction worker that was standing behind a utility truck. When the van came to a stop, Angelo, opened the back doors to the van. From her advantage, Oksana peeked through the luggage and watched as the men slid the upright case to the back of the van. They removed the unconscious First Lady from the case then transferred her to a padded tool cabinet that had been modified to hold her.

"Wait!" Niles said.

Niles reached into the upright case, pulled out a small box, and tossed it in with the First Lady. With a bit of sarcasm, Niles added, "You don't want to forget this."

The men then closed the doors and put the tool cabinet in the back of utility truck.

Angelo was now the man in charge at this end. "Niles, stay with the van. Tonight, when it's clear, take it down to the river and burn everything."

Niles nodded in the affirmative.

On top of the van, Oksana tucked her head down and stayed low. She was able to hear everything.

Angelo turned to the truck driver, Evans, "We're on a tight schedule. When you're done here, meet me across the street."

Angelo drove the utility truck out from under the canopy. Niles went around the van and released the four polls that were holding up the tent. He watched as the canopy fell and covered the tour van.

On top of the van, Oksana waited for Niles to finish what he was doing and walk away before she cautiously shimmied across the luggage. She used her foot and found the ladder that was attached to the back of the van and climbed down. Oksana crouched and quietly slipped under the edge the tarp. As she did, she found herself standing right behind Niles who was having a smoke and was on his cell phone listening to someone on the other end of a conversation.

"Yeah, my end of the job is almost done here." Niles took a drag off his cigarette. "No, but I have some used band equipment I can sell ya." He took another drag, "Oh, I don't know. How about two grand. A saxophone? I don't know, let me check." Niles turned around and pulled back the tarp to look at the cases on top of the van. "Hold on." Niles flicked his cigarette off into the distance and then climbed up the ladder to look through the cases.

Niles' cigarette was smoldering on a small patch of mud that was suddenly put out when Oksana stepped on it as she made her way around a couple of large crates marked HVAC to stay out of sight.

Eventually, Oksana made her way to the end of the row and saw Evans standing outside a flatbed truck that was blocking the entrance to the storage lot.

*****

Inside Air Force One Dalton was on the phone, "What do you mean you don't have a signal?"

Inside the Secret Service car, agents Weller and Lynch were occupying the front seats.

Weller was on the radio to the president, "I'm looking at the screen, Sir. We have no signal. They must be using a jamming device of some kind."

On Air Force One, Dalton was looking at the same security app on his screen. There were three icons. One was marked, Merlin, and it showed his location on Air Force One. He then clicked on, Majestic, and there was no reference to her location. He switched back and forth a couple of times to make sure it wasn't a glitch.

Dalton knew he needed a plan, "Put Morrell on the phone."

Agent Weller had his reservations but passed his phone into the back seat, "The President would like to talk to you."

Kyle took the phone, "Yes sir."

Inside Air Force One, Dalton closed his laptop and then motioned for the female Secret Service agent, Malone, to leave the room. Agent Malone closed the door behind her.

"Kyle, you know that team we're putting together? Discretion is off the table. Go wherever the clues lead you and find Jillian."

Kyle's heart took a leap from his chest into his throat. He had an order from the President of the United States. "Yes, Sir."

"And Kyle" Dalton reiterated, "This is on a need to know basis and unless you hear it directly from me, these orders do not change. If you need anything, just ask."

From the back seat of the Secret Service car, Kyle looked at Aiko. Aiko took his hand. "Yes, sir." After a pause, "Sir, can you pull up the location for Red Butterfly?"

From Dalton's laptop inside Air Force One, Dalton opened the tracking app and click on the icon for Red Butterfly. "Isn't Oksana with you?"

Before Kyle could reply, a locator signal was in a fixed position on the map.

"I have her on 82nd just off airport way."

CHAPTER 4

Oksana stepped out from the storage lot onto the sidewalk and looked in both directions. She saw Evans outside the flatbed looking the other way and quickly ducked back into cover.

As the Secret Service car passed 82nd St., Aiko saw what looked to be Oksana near the corner of a parking structure, "Go back! Turn the car around."

"What is it Aiko?" Kyle replied.

"I just saw Oksana!"

Agent Weller saw a break in the traffic, cut the wheel hard, crossed over two lanes, and made the U-turn. The tires on the Secret Service car tired spun hard against the pavement as it slid sideways for a moment until the car got full traction and was able to straighten out.

Evans, the driver of the flatbed, heard the distant squeal of tires and looked back towards Airport Way when he saw the Secret Service vehicle coming his direction.

From her position, Oksana saw the utility truck pull up on the other side of the flatbed.

From inside the utility truck, Angelo yelled, "Let's go! Move the truck."

As Evans was watching the Secret Service vehicle approach, he replied over his walkie-talkie, "Hold on. We might have company."

Angelo replied back over his radio, "Get rid of them and let me out. We are already behind schedule."

As the Secret Service car drove up 82nd, they could see on one side of the street was the four-story parking structure. It had an overflow storage lot next to it. On the other side of the street, was a construction site where a new hotel was being built.

The construction site's hammerhead crane stood roughly 250 feet in the air, towering over the site. The crane's yellow jib arm had a pallet of drywall on the end of its hook and was in the process of raising construction materials up to the top floor.

Kyle pointed toward the construction worker that was standing by a flatbed truck. "Drop me off here next to this guy."

*****

The Secret Service vehicle stopped across the street from the gates of the construction site on 82nd St. Kyle and Aiko got out of the car. Kyle approached the truck driver, "Have you seen a girl about 15 years old in the last few minutes?"

Evans played his part. "Yeah, when I asked her what she was doing here, she headed across the street and up the sidewalk."

Kyle and Aiko walked across the street to the construction site. The gate to the cyclone fence was locked. Kyle called over a couple of workers from the site.

"Have any of you seen a 15-year-old girl around here in the last few minutes?"

The men working the site look at one another as if someone else had the answer but no one spoke up.

*****

Oksana made her way along the wall of the storage lot trying to stay low and out of sight. Near the entrance to the lot was an open storage bin filled with protective gear. Oksana was able to get close enough without being seen and took out a workman's vest and hardhat. She then slipped back behind the HVAC crates first put on the vest, then the tattered hardhat, where she made sure to tuck her hair all up inside the hat. Oksana heard someone coming and moved back even further behind a set of stacked pallets. On the other side of the pallet stack, a construction worker leaned a STOP/SLOW traffic sign against a honeypot and went inside.

Niles had finished covering up the tour van and joined Angelo at the utility truck. "What's the holdup?"

"Feds."

Niles climbed into the passenger seat of the utility truck, "How can that be?"

"No reason to panic. They've got nothing. They're grasping at straws."

*****

Oksana had noticed the hinge for the honeypot swinging freely when the man had gone inside. She saw there was a small wedge of wood loose on the end of one of the pallets and pulled it off. She then calmly walked up to the side of the honeypot and slipped the latch closed that was used to lock up the portable bathroom up at night and put the stick in the latch. She then quietly took the STOP/SLOW sign and used it as a shield to block her face as she slipped in behind the utility truck.

*****

The workers took their time unlocking the gate to the construction site and let Kyle, Aiko, and the Secret Service agents in to take a look around. The agents quickly fanned out to look for any trace of the First Lady or Oksana. Kyle's focus was on a few guys hanging around in the back of a Dodge 3500 with its tailgate down, unloading drywall. Kyle examined the soft dirt around the site and only saw large boot prints with no sign of Oksana.

*****

Back across the street, Evans was sitting behind the wheel of the flatbed that was blocking the storage lot.

Angelo's voice came over the radio, "We can't wait any longer. Move the truck and I'll head to the top floor of the parking structure. Keep an eye on our friends across the street and have Hector pick me up there."

Evans moved the truck back and kept an eye on the agents across the street. Just as Angelo put the truck in gear, Oksana could hear the construction worker inside the honeypot trying to get out. She quickly sat her small frame down on the back of the utility truck's bumper. She got as prone as she could with the sign between her and the tailgate. With one hand on the bumper and the other the top end of the tailgate she held on as best she could. Angelo drove the utility truck slowly out of the lot and turned up the street toward the entrance of the parking structure.

As Evans was keeping an eye out for more trouble, he turned his attention to the agents across the street and never saw Oksana hanging onto the back of the utility truck as it turned into the parking structure.

*****

Just as the truck turned into the pay by the hour parking superstructure, the truck hit a speed bump, and Oksana lost her grip and fell off. She landed hard on her back and saw the traffic control sign whirling, coming right at her. Out of self-preservation, she caught the sign

26

with two hands and kept it from hitting the ground and making a noise.

The utility truck immediately made a turn and headed up the ramp. Angelo, in his haste, never saw Oksana lying on the ground.

Oksana got up and dusted herself off. She laid the head of the sign across the cement parking stop and stepped firmly on the pole snapping off the sign. She grabbed the wooden pole that was about the size of a solid broom handle and started to run up the ramp following the utility truck, making sure to stay far enough back as not to be seen.

*****

Just as Kyle and Aiko left the construction site, he heard the squealing tires of the utility truck as it drove up the ramps of the parking structure.

Kyle motioned to Aiko, "Follow me."

Kyle and Aiko ran across 82nd St. and into the parking structure followed by agents Weller and Lynch.

Both Kyle and Aiko stopped just as they entered the parking structure when they saw the sigh that had been snapped off lying on the ground. Kyle drew his weapon and motioned for Aiko to stay behind him. Agents Weller and Lynch had followed Kyle and Aiko into the parking structure. Aiko tapped Kyle on the shoulder, motioned to the stairwell, and started to head in that direction.

Kyle turned to the agents," Take the ramps while Aiko and I take stairs."

The teams split up.

A minute later when Evans entered the parking structure, both teams were out of sight. He saw the end of the broken traffic sign and paused trying to decide whether to take the stairs or the ramp.

*****

The utility truck drove up the last ramp and onto the top level of the four-story parking structure that had no roof. Angelo parked in an open slot with no cars on either side, away from any free-standing light poles.

"Now what?" Niles asked.

"We wait."

Angelo adjusted his side mirror to focus over the edge of the parking wall in the direction of the hotel being constructed across the street.

Niles was getting impatient. "What are we waiting for?"

"Not to worry. I have a contingency plan in place. Help is on the way."

Niles couldn't sit still and needed another cigarette. He got out of the truck to light up.

Oksana was running up the ramps looking for the utility truck. When she was halfway up the last ramp, she saw the back of utility truck and slipped behind a parked car for cover.

Angelo got out of the truck, reached back onto the seat, and grabbed the walkie-talkie. "We need to make an adjustment. Pick us up across the street, top floor."

Niles was calming down but still a bit paranoid as he continued to scan the area. He looked down the ramp and saw Oksana peeking over the hood of a car. Without giving away he had noticed her, he nodded his head slightly to one side in the direction of the down ramp. "We've got company."

"Go check it out."

Niles crushed out his cigarette, reached into the back of the truck, and pulled back a tarp. Under the tarp was a long leather case. Niles slipped out a double-barreled shotgun from its padded sleeve. He cracked the breach open and saw that both barrels were loaded, then closed the breach and headed down the ramp.

CHAPTER 5

Oksana saw Niles coming, got low, then circled up and around a couple of cars. She could hear his heavy footsteps as he made his way down the ramp. Oksana worked her way to the back of the cars to slip around to the other side but found that both cars were parked tightly up near the cement retaining wall. Niles' footsteps were getting louder and reverberating the deeper he got into the structure.

Oksana laid down flat and saw she had a better chance to slither under the bumper of a 4X4 then the car. She worked her way between the wall and the cement stop. She had to move quickly, and at the same time not let the pole hit the metal on the truck as not to give away her position. Once under the width of the front bumper, Oksana reached the pole above her head and laid it on the ground. Using both hands she grabbed the end of the bumper and pulled the rest of her body out from under the front of the truck.

As Niles got closer to where he last saw Oksana, he led with the shotgun. When he got there, he did not see her.

Niles knelt and took a quick look under the car that was on the upside of the ramp and saw nothing. He then got to his hands and knees and peeked under the car on the downhill side of the ramp. Nothing.

As Niles dropped to his hands and knees, Oksana carefully and quietly, sat up on the edge of a car with her feet off the ground. She sat there listening for a moment. Then she heard Niles start to scuffle to his feet and she lowered herself back down to the pavement between the set of cars that were only two rows away.

As Niles stood he saw no sign of Oksana, but what he did see was a stairwell nearby, and started to head in that direction. He looked to the left, all clear. A quick look behind him. All clear. As he turned back to the front, Oksana sprung out with momentum, cracked him across the wrist with the staff forcing him to drop the shotgun.

Niles tried to go for the shotgun, but Oksana started in with a barrage of a beat down with the wooden pole. Oksana wielded it like the wooden bokuto training sword that Aiko had taught her to use. Oksana came down with a solid crack to Niles' rib cage. She held onto the end of the pole with both hands and she rested the other end of the pole on Niles' battered torso.

Kyle and Aiko appeared outside of the stairwell. The momentary distraction caused Oksana to pause. Niles grabbed the end of the pole and he and Oksana fought for possession as he made his way to his feet. Once Niles had better leverage, he swung Oksana around, and the momentum caused her to lose her grip and she was sent stumbling backward in Kyle and Aiko's direction. Aiko stepped forward and caught Oksana before she lost all control.

Niles in retaliation whipped the pole through the air at Aiko. Aiko shifted Oksana to the side and caught the pole without missing a beat. Aiko regripped her hands and stepped forward with complete confidence.

Aiko looked Niles straight in the eye, showing no fear. Niles saw Aiko like no woman he had ever come up against. Aiko repositioned the wooden pole a few times to get a feel for how Niles was going to react. He reacted by taking a step back and looking around to reassess his options.

Niles took another step back and stepped on the stock of his shotgun. He knew what it was without having to look down. Still holding eye contact, Aiko knew her opponent was going to have to go for the shotgun to have a chance, as did Niles. Niles let his eyes wander over to Kyle to see if Aiko would look as well, she did not. When Niles looked back at Aiko, it was like a switch went off. As Niles dropped to go for the shotgun, Aiko stepped forward and with a quick, solid blow, cracked Niles across the side of the ribs as he reached for the weapon.

With his left arm, Niles caught the wooden staff under his arm and gripped the pole with his hand. With his right hand, he grabbed the only part of the shotgun he could, the barrel. Aiko kicked Niles in the left elbow that was pinning the pole to his side, driving the staff deeper into his ribs. Niles loosened his grip and Aiko was able to withdraw the four-foot pole.

As Niles got to his feet, he swung the shotgun around by the barrel trying to catch Aiko with the butt end. Aiko saw it coming, took a slight step back, and let the gun's momentum pass on by her. Aiko countered with a strike to Niles' right elbow.

The pain was so intense Niles couldn't even catch his breath to scream. As he let go of the barrel of the shotgun with his right hand he felt the weight of the gun in his left. Like flipping a baseball bat, he flipped the shotgun end-to-end and caught the gun in the middle. Aiko took another step, closing the distance, so she was inside the length of the shotgun's barrel.

She took the pole in her left hand and gripped the gun's barrel under her left arm as she punched Niles in the face while still holding onto the pole.

Niles pitched backward, his hand slid back and as it did, he was able to regrip at the trigger. His finger caught the lead trigger causing the shotgun to fire off one of the 12-gauge rounds.

Kyle and Oksana were far enough to one side that neither one of them was hit. Aiko could feel the heat from the barrel between her arm and her body causing her to relax her arm's grip, and that gave Niles a chance to take control of the shotgun. Before Niles could raise the shotgun, Aiko regripped the pole with both hands that she was now holding vertically in front of Niles. With two quick moves, Aiko first pivoted the pole at the bottom, cracking Niles in the groin, then back the other way striking him in his forehead. Dazed, Niles dropped the shotgun and stumbled backward. Aiko took a step forward and while keeping her eye on Niles, she stepped on the shotgun and slid it back behind her with her foot, and it came to a stop between her and Kyle.

Even after hearing the shotgun blast, Angelo stayed with the utility truck because the priority was the First Lady. He knew time was running out and was relieved when he saw a large round shadow moving across the pavement in his direction. He looked up as he went to his radio. "It's about time."

Down the ramp from the utility truck, Aiko held Niles at bay as she tried to keep herself between Niles and Oksana who was standing next to Kyle. Oksana reached down and went to pick up the shotgun.

Kyle reached out. "No Oksana."

Aiko's concern for Oksana gave away her advantage as she took a quick look back at her young protege. It was just long enough for Niles to reach out and grab the other end of the pole. Aiko felt the tension and turned back toward Niles as he made his move. Niles lunged, and Aiko countered, but in doing so, got too close and Niles was able to grab Aiko by her wrist. Niles raised her hand above her head and pushed his body into hers, forcing her to do a half turn, and now she had her back to her opponent. In doing so, the pole ended up between them as they still each had a grip on the wooden shaft.

Niles thought it would be an advantage to let go of the pole and put his left arm around Aiko's throat. Oksana made eye contact with Aiko and she knew just what Aiko was about to do because she and Aiko had done this at home, in their make-shift dojo, many times. Oksana smiled.

Aiko dropped the pole, grabbed Niles' wrist that was to her throat, and dropped her weight. As Aiko's body dropped its lower center of gravity, she shifted her head to one side and kicked up with her right foot. One second Niles was standing, the next, Aiko's foot had kicked up to the side of his head, and he went down hard.

Aiko spun free. Niles not only felt the pain in his jaw, he also felt the pole he landed on and it acted like a wheel, which caused him to roll to one side, flopping on the ground like a fish out of water. Niles got his bearings, picked up the stick, and came at Aiko with all the rage he had.

Niles raised the staff above his head as he charged Aiko. Before he could reverse the backswing downward, Aiko took two quick steps in and hit Niles right below the ribcage with such precision, it caused Niles to almost freeze in that position.

Aiko danced around Niles before he could come out of his temporary paralysis and stood ready to continue should he try again. Suddenly, Niles had his air back in his body and he folded over for a second. Then he looked at the pole as if to say to himself that he was the one who was supposed to have the advantage.

In his weakened state, he thought he had a chance and turned toward Aiko. Even standing in all that free space, he felt like a cornered animal. He regripped the pole and took his best shot. Aiko reminded him he was no match. Aiko threw three punches in such quick succession to Niles' solar plexus, he lost his grip on the pole and Aiko caught it right out of the air as if she already knew it was going to happen.

Niles had one last burst of adrenaline left in him. He grabbed Aiko by the wrist of the arm that she was holding the pole in and used the last of his strength to lift Aiko's arm up in the air. Aiko saw the fire sprinkler system above her on the ceiling and was able to flick her wrist and strike the sprinkler with the end of the pole, setting off the sprinkler.

The shock of the water startled her assailant momentarily giving Aiko a slight advantage to escape his grasp, but in the process, she dropped the pole and stepped back closer to Kyle and Oksana. Niles looked at Kyle and Aiko and noticed they were no longer interested in the fight. They were now looking past him, up the ramp. Niles turned and saw what they were looking at. A large ball with a hook hovering over the utility truck.

Oksana used the distraction to run past Niles and up the ramp toward utility truck.

*****

Angelo grabbed onto the hook, just below the spherical metal ball that was dangling from the end of the crane's fully extended arm. He attached it to the top of the reinforced metal loop in the middle of the rack of the utility truck. He jumped out of the bed of the truck, going over the side and got on his radio as he climbed in behind the wheel. He was calling for the crane operator as Oksana reached the truck. "Ready. Let's go."

Just before the truck started to lift, Oksana grabbed onto the back of the truck and climbed in next to the case that held the First Lady.

Oksana saw there were two metal twist latches that each were locked with a medium sized padlock. She grabbed a large flathead screwdriver out of a tool pouch and started trying to pry open one of the locks.

*****

Niles knew he was in a losing fight going hand-to-hand with Aiko, but he had to do whatever he could to give Angelo more time to escape. He took a stance as if to say, you got to get past me if you want the First Lady. Aiko stepped up and with a crushing blow to his throat

37

and he stumbled in no real direction. He looked up and saw the exit to the stairwell, and alongside it, a fire extinguisher box. Niles forced himself over to the box, threw his elbow into it, and removed the fire extinguisher.

Aiko rushed Niles before he could pull the pin. Niles panicked and in turn, threw the fire extinguisher at Aiko. She ducked, and the extinguisher skipped across the cement floor and started to roll up the ramp.

Aiko turned to avoid a direct hit from the extinguisher and in doing so saw that the truck Oksana was in was starting to rise into the air. Aiko ran toward the ramp, grabbed the extinguisher that was now rolling back in her direction, and tossed it back toward her assailant.

As the extinguisher was in midflight Aiko yelled, "Kyle!"

Aiko continued to run up the ramp to try to get to Oksana before the truck was too high to reach.

Out of reflexes, Niles caught the extinguisher. Before he could decide what to do with it he found himself staring down the barrel of the shotgun Kyle was now pointing in his direction. Niles was like a deer frozen in the headlights and could not let go of the extinguisher. Kyle fired the second 12-gauge round from the shotgun, hitting the metal casing of the fire extinguisher. The extinguisher exploded sending pieces of shrapnel into Niles, killing him instantly. Niles was blown off his feet and as he landed, he was lost in a cloud of white fire retardant.

CHAPTER 6

Oksana was in the back of the utility truck and had the end of the long screwdriver in the loop of the lock. She was using all the leverage she could muster to get it to open. The lock was holding but she saw the weakened loop in the latch on the case was giving way. She could hear Aiko yelling, telling her to get out of the back of the truck just as she was about to get the latch open. "Oksana! Jump!"

Oksana was frantically working the lock when the latch gave way, and she popped the first lock. "I almost have her!"

Oksana started to go for the second latch when she could feel the truck being lifted completely off the ground and she lost her balance.

Aiko was too late to help Oksana as the truck was now 10 feet in the air. Kyle ran up behind Aiko.

Oksana could not hold her position. She dropped the screwdriver and slid back hard against the inside of the tailgate, causing the tailgate to pop open. Oksana slid out onto the lowered tailgate causing the truck to be out of balance.

The truck tilted, and Oksana was forced to roll out of the back of the truck. As she did, she grabbed onto the top edge of the tailgate and was now dangling on the back of the truck. Oksana pulled herself up onto her elbows and saw the utility belt had slid out onto the hinge area of the tailgate. Sticking out from under the tool pouch was the large screwdriver she had been using to pry the locks from the case. The hook holding the truck shifted and the case holding the First Lady started to slide backward.

Oksana saw the case start to slide her way. She grabbed the large screwdriver and jammed the end of it into the hinge area of the tailgate. The case slid back and stopped up against the screwdriver. Oksana was still holding onto the handle of the screwdriver and the case hit with such force, it pinches her fingers between the handle and the side of the case.

Oksana's reaction was to quickly pull her hand out and in doing so caused her to shift her weight to one side. The truck tilted again causing the loose items to tumble out the back. Oksana tried to shift her weight forward and grabbed the handle on the side of the case. As she did, she was forced back and her attempt to grab the handle failed.

Gravity was winning, and she felt her momentum sliding backward. All she had a chance to do was control how she went off the back of the truck. When she went over she was able to get one good grip on the top edge of the tailgate with her left hand. As she dangled, her body swung away from the truck and then back, and that was when she reached up and grabbed the top of the tailgate with her right hand.

Oksana was once again dangling off the back of the tailgate by just her fingertips. The items that tumbled out of the truck fell five stories to the street below. Oksana was losing her grip.

The screwdriver holding the case back shifted a little but still held. Oksana knew from her training with Aiko you can only control what you can control. Oksana could feel her fingers weakening. She looked out in front of her and saw the back bumper and the ball hitch. She didn't have time to think as she lost her grip with her left hand and then her right. She threw her hands forward and grabbed onto the ball of the truck's trailer hitch.

Kyle and Aiko were joined by agents Weller and Lynch. Kyle turned to the agents. "You guys head back down to the construction site."

The agents retreated toward the stairwell.

Oksana dangled high above 82nd St. as the jig arm of the crane swung her and the truck from the parking garage's exposed top floor into the construction site across the street.

Kyle and Aiko ran down the ramp back toward the stairwell. Kyle stopped and checked for an ID on what was left of Niles' body. He found what was left of a construction badge and pulled it from the lanyard that was looped around Niles' neck.

*****

Kyle and Aiko had worked their way down the stairwell between the third and fourth floor and stopped to look out the gap to see where the crane was planning to lower the truck. All they could do was watch as

Oksana frantically continued to hold onto the back of the truck's hitch.

*****

At the construction site, the men nearest the back of the truck that held the drywall stopped their efforts of unloading the drywall when they looked and saw Oksana dangling from the back of the utility truck. Two sheets of drywall that were taped together were now leaning from the edge of the tailgate to the ground.

As the crane operator got the truck close to the space just above the truck with the drywall, Oksana was able to look down over her shoulder and saw a stack of insulation near the truck. She knew she couldn't hold on any longer and kicked her legs out in the direction of the insulation and let go. The truck's teetering didn't work in Oksana's favor and she missed her mark when she fell the 15 feet to the ground. Instead of hitting the insulation she landed on the slant of the leaning drywall. It broke her fall, but it also shattered the drywall into pieces.

Oksana was laid out on the ground covered by chunks of drywall. She felt the pain all over her body and she could hardly move. Her head was pounding and the ringing in her ears was an inconsistent blend of ever-changing frequencies. The last thing she remembered before passing out was a couple of very unhappy construction workers finding her under the crumpled pieces of drywall, that were laced together by an odd-looking strand of yellow cord.

*****

From the stairwell, Kyle and Aiko watched as two of the construction workers peeled the chunks of drywall away from Oksana while another guided the truck to the open space on the ground. As the truck landed, Angelo got out and joined the other men to quickly get the tool case that held the First Lady off the back of the truck.

One of the workers asked, "What are we going to do with the girl?"

Angelo made the call. "Open the case."

The construction team opened the case containing the First Lady. Angelo removed some of the padded insulation and then they stuffed Oksana into the case along with the First Lady. Angelo stuck some of the padded insulation around Oksana and closed the case.

Angelo knew they didn't have much time. "Get me the assets."

One of the workers reached in behind the seat of the truck and pulled out a small duffle bag. Angelo opened the bag and removed bundles of cash that had been wrapped in cellophane. Angelo opened a drawer in the bottom of the case, added the bundles of cash into the drawer, then closed the drawer.

Kyle and Aiko saw two construction workers run out from the parking structure's entrance below them and crossed the street toward the construction site. Kyle and Aiko ran down the stairs to the ground floor entrance.

Agents Weller and Lynch were found in a daze lying on the ground at the bottom of stairs.

Kyle knelt to check on the two agents. "I think they are going to be okay."

Kyle looked up at Aiko and saw a third man come out of the shadows and reach out for Aiko.

"Aiko!"

Aiko could not react fast enough. The man grabbed her from behind with a bear hug. Aiko dropped her weight and slipped through his arms as Kyle lunged at the man. Aiko rolled out of the way. Kyle and the assailant exchanged a couple of blows. Out in front of Aiko was the top part of the STOP/SLOW sign.

Kyle took a hard shot to the gut and when he came up his head caught his opponent in the chin. The blow had the man just about out on his feet. His weakened legs took the momentum his brain had created from the spinning effect and turned his body around to face Aiko. Aiko had a solid grip on what was left of the handle and swung the sign like it was an eighteen-inch sword and sliced the man's throat clean back to the spine. The man only had enough time to grab his throat as he fell to the ground before his body even realized he was dead.

Kyle and Aiko were about to exit the garage and cross the street when they saw two more Secret Service cars speeding up the street toward them. Kyle ran out into the road and pointed to the gate of the construction site. The lead car turned and crashed through the locked gate.

Kyle and Aiko followed the second car in and found the Secret Service agents had already exited their cars and had the construction workers at bay.

Aiko looked where Oksana and the First Lady should have been and only saw broken pieces of drywall and white dust on the ground.

Aiko felt a pain she had never known before and let out a scream. "Oksana!"

Kyle and Aiko quickly searched the area around the truck before looking up just in time to see a black case with a chrome frame. It was 40 feet in the air, held by a set of straps that looped into the crane's hook, being lifted over a wall to the opposite side of the construction site.

Kyle motioned to the agents, "Secure this site. We'll go after the case."

Kyle and Aiko ran off the construction site, down the sidewalk, and around the corner.

CHAPTER 7

Two 40-foot eighteen wheelers were parked parallel, ten feet apart in the lot of the adjoining hotel. The trucks were backed in toward the wall as the case was being brought over. In the space between them, was an old pickup truck facing outward. The pickup truck had its tailgate down and was ready to receive the case. The case was guided and lowered into place on the dropped tailgate by two men dressed as dock workers.

The driver of the truck, Javier, had on a radio headset and was in communication with the crane operator. His helper, Milo, unhooked the straps and freed up the case to slide it into the back of the pickup. Once the case was secure Javier took off the headset and tossed it into the back of the truck. The pickup was disguised to look like a truck full of old used tires which had a false lower half.

The two men pushed the case into the prepared space as far as it would go, placed a few loose tires behind it, and closed the tailgate. As far as it looked, it was just a truck full of old used tires going off to be recycled.

Kyle and Aiko came running around the corner up the side of the hotel. They stopped and tried to catch their breath as they looked for where the case would have cleared the wall.

Aiko shook her head. "I don't see anything."

Kyle pointed up the road and they started walking. "Up there. Beyond those semis."

A truck was heading their way. Kyle took a glancing look into the back of the truck carrying old tires as it drove past them.

Kyle and Aiko reached the area between the two semis and all they saw were the straps that once held the case suspended from the hook, lying on the ground.

Kyle checked his phone to make sure it was on the right channel.

"Sir, they have FLOTUS."

There was a long pause. Kyle could see the loss in Aiko's eyes.

"There's more."

*****

Dalton was at his desk listening on the other end of the secure cell phone. He was calm, but there was a change in his demeanor.

Kyle took another deep breath. "Sir, they have Oksana, too." Kyle was cautious, "I may have a couple of leads…"

"What leads? Tell me who did this!"

"We have a few of the crewmen and the name of the construction company they used to pull this off. Do you know of anyone who would want to do this?"

Dalton was on his feet pacing. He looked through the interior of the cabin of Air Force One from his office. Personnel were on their phones reaching out to their contacts, trying to get any lead to report to their Commander in Chief.

Dalton closed the door for privacy. "I want you to get everything you can on this Kyle. If it takes getting dirty, so be it, and when you have something solid for us to go on, report back to me. Me only. We might be compromised. Do you copy?"

*****

Kyle and Aiko were making their way back to the construction site.

"Yes, Sir." Kyle hung up the phone.

"Kyle." Aiko's voice carried her pain.

"Yes."

"I'm scared."

"Please don't be afraid, Aiko. We're going to get through this and I need you to be strong. Knowing that gives me strength."

"I thought you were not afraid of anything."

"I wasn't until I met you."

"I don't understand."

"There's only one thing that scares me."

Kyle and Aiko stopped walking. Aiko looked up into Kyle's eyes.

Kyle continued, "Losing you would be the worst thing that could ever happen to me."

Kyle took Aiko in his arms. When he felt Aiko's arms embrace him, he knew there was going to be nothing that would stop them from finding the man who was responsible for taking Oksana.

"Kyle-san."

"Yes, Aiko."

"I will give my last dying breath to bring Oksana back to us."

Kyle understood and felt the same way. He took Aiko by the hand and started walking back to the construction site. As they made their way to the entrance they saw that the Secret Service agents had all the construction workers in plastic hand ties going over all of the identifications and cross-checking them through the criminal database.

Kyle saw the construction workers were all crammed into the back of one of the pickups. They were sitting on top of six pieces of drywall that were laid flat in the back of the truck. They sat shoulder to shoulder and were a bit more skittish than the regular group of accomplices. The Secret Service agents were talking on their coms as Kyle and Aiko approached.

The lead agent, Agent Stevens, turned to Kyle. "We got the word to give you full access. Personally, I think you should be off this case as you two might be too close to this to act in a rational manner."

"Maybe, or the president thinks it's going to take more than a rational manner to get the two people you were in charge of, back?"

A couple of the captured construction workers chuckled under their breath. Kyle asked the Secret Service agent closest to the back of the truck, "When you searched these guys, did you find anything?"

Agent Randell hesitated. "A few of them had ID's, probably fake. A couple of cell phones and this." Agent Randell held out a small hand-held device with a couple of small lights on it along with a pair of switches.

"Do you have an idea what it goes to?" Kyle asked.

"We can turn it on and find out."

Kyle noticed the group of construction workers being held in the back of the truck began to get a little nervous. Kyle reached out and put his hand over the device the agent was holding. "I think we better hold off on that for now."

Aiko noticed the pieces of crushed drywall that Oksana had landed were in linked together by a piece of yellow cord. The cord ran through them and then over to a piece of the side of the drywall where it was sticking out from under one of the edges. There was a small bump under the edge of the paper that held the two full sheets together during shipment.

Kyle noticed it as well. Kyle pointed to the yellow cord. "What's that?"

The Secret Service agents hadn't yet fully investigated the discrepancy. "What's what?"

"The yellow cord." Kyle gestured, "There."

Agent Randell reached down and grabbed the loose end of the cord and started to pull on it slightly. The construction workers in the back of the truck once again started to stir.

"Stop!" Kyle yelled.

The agent stopped pulling.

Kyle knelt and took a closer look at the cord. "This is primer cord."

Kyle began to follow the cord and saw it was running all through the broken-up sheet of drywall. Kyle cautiously continued to follow the cord and came to a flat remote detonator that was hidden within the edge of the drywall.

"Why would anyone do that?" Agent Randell asked.

Kyle rubbed his fingertip over some of the powder that was loose from the white chalk of the drywall. He tasted the dust off his fingertip then spit out the residue. "Because it's not drywall," Kyle replied.

Aiko had a suspicion but had to ask, "What is it?"

Kyle took a small piece of the chalky substance and crushed it in his hand, grinding it down to a finer powder, and held out his hand to show Aiko. "Cocaine."

CHAPTER 8

Dalton was on the phone as he sat at his desk on Air Force One.

"Plans have changed. I need you here now. I have the girl, too."

******

The pickup truck filled with old tires that held the case containing FLOTUS and Oksana was approaching the shipping yard along the Willamette River when it hit a deep pothole in the roadway.

Inside the insulated case, the heavy jarring made the cramped quarters even more uncomfortable. Oksana was a bit jacked up from inhaling the cocaine dust and felt something jab her leg when they hit the pothole.

Oksana reached down as far as she could and felt something with her fingertips. It was the frequency jamming device. Her outstretched hand flicked the trigger and momentarily turned it off.

At the shipyard, the older of the two, Javier, backed the truck up behind a shipping container. The younger man, Milo, got out of the truck and opened the back doors of the container. Javier then backed the truck to the backend of the open container. Unlike the others, this container had no official destination and papers.

Inside the case, Oksana was still fidgeting with the device that poked her leg and, in the process, hit the trigger and turned the jamming device back on.

*****

On Air Force One, Dalton was pacing as best he could in what little office space he had. With each passing minute, the suite seemed to be getting smaller, adding to the anxiety that came with the job. There was a knock at the door.

"Come in."

Agent Malone entered. "Sir, we might have a lead. We just had a momentary signal and a partial from another signal. It could be FLOTUS and Oksana, Sir."

"What do you mean, momentarily?"

"It was only for about 30 seconds, but we were able to triangulate it enough to put her downtown along the river. Our best guess would be either the shipping yard below the Fremont Bridge or the train station."

"Has Casey arrived?"

"Yes, Sir."

"Send him in."

"Will there be anything else, Sir?"

"No. Thank you, Sienna, that will be all."

Agent Malone went on with her duties. A moment later there was another knock at the door.

"Enter."

Casey entered and closed the door behind him.

Dalton gestured, "Take a seat."

Casey sat down across from Dalton.

Dalton continued, "I need you to take your team down to the shipyard and try to locate two signals and find out if one of them is really FLOTUS."

"Two signals?"

"Yes, two signals. They might have Oksana as well."

"And if it is them?" Casey asked.

"Nothing's changed. Rendezvous at NuFa 23 as planned."

*****

Javier and Milo had to do their job and nothing else. Don't do anything to draw attention. The two of them dropped the tailgate, removed excess tires, and pulled the trunk from its concealment. They each took a handle and unloaded the case that was practically twice as heavy as expected. Milo got in behind the wheel of the truck and drove it around to the other side of the container where they had a second vehicle waiting.

Milo switched over to a black van with its back and side windows blacked out. On the side of the van were decals that read, Multnomah Vector Control along with a bogus phone number. Milo backed the van around to the open end of the of the container. He drove in deep enough to center it and then they closed the outside doors in front of the van. Milo had left the headlights on so there was light inside the container.

Javier opened the back of the van and as Milo joined him, together they each took a handle to load the case into the back of the black van completing the switch. Just as they were about to lift the case, they felt a hard kick from inside. As Javier turned and reached into the back of the van for something, Milo opened the case.

Javier tried to warn Milo, but it was too late. "Milo, Wait!"

Milo had already opened the case. Oksana immediately kicked Milo in the chest sending him backward. Javier reached in with a cattle prod and zapped Oksana into submission.

Oksana rubbed out the spot where she had been tased and focused her hatred on Javier. "Asshole."

Javier held up the end of the cattle prod. "You want a fresh one?"

Oksana awkwardly tried to climb out of the case. The look on her captors' faces told her they weren't going to help her get to her feet. Once out, she reached down and helped Jillian get out of the confines of the trunk. The two men noticed that Jillian had wet herself while sedated. Javier went to the back of the van, reached in for a small duffel bag, and tossed it at Jillian's feet.

Javier was looking forward to the next few minutes with the First Lady. "Take off your clothes."

"No!"

Javier held the cattle prod up and put it up close to Jillian's butt cheek. Jillian held her ground. Javier wanted his pleasure and part of that was pain. He touched the end of the cattle prod to Jillian's ass cheek. He could feel Jillian tense up as she was expecting a jolt, but Javier just continued to rub the end of the prod over her ass. Although he was not physically touching her, Jillian could feel his filth on her. She could see it in his eyes. She knew if she did not comply, that he might take out his anger on Oksana.

Jillian turned around thinking, "Let's just get this over with," and dropped her dress.

Javier let the end of the prod run along Jillian's hip as she turned, like it was an extension of his hand. He ran the end of the rod up along her spine as he admired what great shape she was in. He stuck the end of the prod up under the edge of the clasp on the back of her bra. He played with her. Jillian was getting just a small sense of what the girls she was trying to protect with her foundation must have to go through before being traded or sold on the dark web.

Jillian did her best to take her head out of the equation. Jillian brushed back the prod and undid her bra. She caught it in her crossed arms, not allowing it to fall.

Javier wasn't satisfied, he wanted more. "All of it."

The words, "Just get it over with," kept running through Jillian's mind as she tried to slip her panties down with one hand. Javier jabbed the end of the cattle prod into the back of Jillian's hand and gave it a small zap.

Oksana about jumped out of her skin.

Jillian held out her scorched hand. "Don't Oksana!"

Oksana held her ground and pushed away Milo's hand as he tried to keep her back.

Jillian gave Javier a hard look showing the fire in her eyes. Jillian was mainly thinking of Oksana when she did what had to be done to save her. Jillian let her bra fall to the ground as she slipped her fingers into the elastic of her panties. She tried not to show Oksana the fear that was going on inside her, but her trembling hands gave her away as dropped her panties to the floor.

The men let her stand there in humiliation for a moment. The cool night air gave Jillian goose bumps across her skin as Javier rubbed the edge of the metal cattle prod against her. Javier held the other end of the prod between his legs like it was an extension of his manhood.

Milo looked at Oksana and saw what innocence she might have left in her and thought she might have seen enough and offered Javier a way out. "There's a set of sweats in the bag."

Oksana went for the bag to help her.

Javier pointed the cattle prod at Oksana to suggest she better keep her distance or she was next. Javier played every prick card he had in the deck. "She's a big girl, she can do it herself."

Jillian still had her back to the men and slowly squatted down, reached behind her, and grabbed the bag. She pulled out the jacket first, which was a little big, and put it on. The length of the jacket just covered her buttock.

Javier gently slipped the cattle prod between Jillian's legs at her knees and started to slowly raise the prod rubbing the inside of one of her thighs.

To Jillian, Javier's voice felt like the grimy filth he was. "After you dress, we are not going to have any more problems, correct?"

Jillian nodded.

The two men had a slight grin still on their faces from the show. Then they looked over at Oksana. Oksana was still feeling the effects of cocaine and was like a mad dog foaming at the mouth.

Javier once again pointed the cattle prod in her direction.

Jillian tried not to bend over too much to keep from exposing herself as she put on the sweatpants. As she got the waistband of the sweats up to her knees, she felt the weight of the prod holding them down. Javier had slipped the prod between her legs and was making it slow and difficult for Jillian to pull them up. The higher she pulled the sweats up the tension increased. She had the sweats up close to her hips and could feel the prod was now between her thighs, with very little room to go before she would feel that cold shaft up as far as it would go.

Jillian had to give in to the degradation in order not to be violated right there in front of Oksana. Jillian let her voice tremble. "Please…"

Javier wanted his point to be made. "Then please me."

Jillian pulled up on the sweats, forcing the shaft near the end of the cattle prod to go up as high as it could go, and it pressed up against her. The metal felt as cold and even worse as Javier slowly began to pull back on the prod.

As soon as the cattle prod cleared the edge of the sweats, the sweats popped up over Jillian's ass cheeks and as she tightened the drawstrings of the sweats she could feel herself start to breathe again.

CHAPTER 9

In the back of the darkened van that was now locked inside the container, FLOTUS and Oksana were strapped into bucket seats like you would find in first class on an airplane. Their hands were zip-tied in front of them.

Milo was sitting in a chair opposite them. He held the signal jamming device in his hand. "I hope you're comfortable. It's going to be a long ride."

Jillian felt like she might get more information out of the younger Milo than Javier who was sitting in the front of the van behind a wall of plexiglass. "Where are you taking us?"

Oksana's senses were in overdrive from the adrenaline rush caused by the cocaine, "Do you have any idea who my father is?"

Jillian did her best to keep Oksana calm. "Oksana, Milo here was going to tell us what this is all about."

Milo knew more than what he could say and did feel sorry for what had happened, but he did not give into the First Lady's ploy. Jillian touched Oksana's knee to stop her from tapping her foot and to let her know she wanted Oksana to calm down.

Jillian tried another way to get Milo talking. "The US government does not pay ransoms."

"This has nothing to do with ransom."

"Then why did you kidnap us?"

Milo looked at Oksana and gave a guilty nod to let Jillian know, "That was never the plan."

Jillian turned to Oksana. Oksana's mind was in another gear and she couldn't understand her confusion but knew she wanted out of her skin and let out a blood-curdling scream. "Ahhhhhh!"

Milo waited for the echo in his head to clear. "Scream all you want. This container is soundproofed, and your tracking devices are jammed so no one will be coming to rescue you."

Oksana was still covered in white powder, anxious like a wild animal. Milo's words had a sobering reality to them and Oksana went quiet.

Jillian looked at Milo and kept her voice down. "What did you do to her?"

"Nothing. She did it to herself."

"What do you mean?"

"She's covered in cocaine. She'll come down soon or…."

Jillian didn't like where this conversation was going. "Or what?"

Milo replied matter-of-factly, "Or die." After a moment Milo continued, "I've seen it happen. When my little sister was twelve she got a hold of a kilo of cocaine that was stashed in our basement. She thought it looked like snow, so she kept throwing it in the air until she had gone through the whole package. In such a small space she ended up inhaling a lot of it and I was the one who found her."

"I'm sorry, Milo." Jillian thought if she could comfort Milo it might get him talking and he might give away something she could use to find out who was behind her kidnapping.

"It was my fault. I left the door to the basement open."

"Were they your drugs? No. So don't let anyone blame you for what happened."

"It doesn't matter now. I've been working off the debt ever since."

"Who do you owe?" Jillian asked.

The container shifted and was starting to be lifted off the ground. From the front of the van, Javier opened the sliding window between the two compartments. "It won't be long now."

Jillian could sense a worst-case scenario coming and tried one more time to reason with her captors. "It's me you want. Let Oksana go."

"I'm afraid that ship has sailed. Looks like for both of you, your services are no longer required." Javier said before closing the sliding window.

This time it wasn't the cocaine, Oksana let out another pent-up scream.

*****

Outside of the shipping container, Oksana's screams could not be heard as the container was lifted onto a flatbed truck. Once the container was secure, the truck began to pull away and headed out of the shipping yard. As the flatbed cleared the gate, Casey's SUV pulled into the thirty-acre shipping yard. The SUV came to a stop where the previous coordinates given to him by the president gave them the best place to start looking. Casey's four-man team exited the vehicle, and they fanned out. Casey was holding a tracking device. He panned around 360° and didn't find a signal. Casey hit a preset number on his cell phone.

"Sir, we have nothing at this location."

Dalton came over the phone. "Head to the next location to pick up the package. We need to stay on schedule."

CHAPTER 10

Outside the George Anthony Studios, a dark Mercedes S-Class sedan stopped in front of the building and Kamiko's assistant, Koji Takata, stepped out of the car carrying a soft leather business briefcase and entered the building.

Once inside, Mr. Takata walked past the studio's latest acquisition that displayed a coral encrusted skeleton. The well-dressed Asian man was greeted by the women who worked the counter.

"How may I be of service to you?"

Takata reached into his pocket and handed the woman a business card. The card read, Marine Science Technologies, LLC.

"My name is Mr. Takata and I believe Mr. Anthony is expecting me."

The woman picked up a cell phone and hit a preset number. "There's a Mr. Takata here to see you."

The woman hung up the cell phone. "If you'd like to wait in the lobby, Mr. Anthony will be right with you."

*****

Takata stood in front of a large fish tank. Inside the tank were the remains of the fully intact Vargas' skeleton. It was still covered in colorful coral, just as it was discovered, then excavated from the shelf in the Sea of Japan. Even the water in the tank was brought over from the Sea of Japan to protect the integrity of the find. Just outside the tank on one side was a brass bell from the ship, The AMADA. On the other side was the wooden mermaid figurehead that was mounted on a false bow of a ship that was connected to the wall. The wood on the maiden had been treated and then covered with several coats of a clear lacquer to keep the air from causing the wood to rot.

As Takata admired the relics he could hear the quickened pace of a fine pair of dress shoes as someone was approaching him from behind.

"The only thing missing is the Monarch Moon," George said.

Takata turned and greeted by Mr. George Anthony. "Yes. Maybe one day."

"But in the meantime, it is my understanding you have something you would like not to be on display.

Mr. Takata nodded.

"Then may I suggest we head to my office."

As the two men walked across the lobby toward George's office, Mr. Takata's phone pinged. He quickly glanced at the message on the display which read, On the way.

*****

Once inside his office, George opened the safe and removed a small box. George handed the box to Mr. Takata who didn't waste any time in opening it. Inside was a large diamond in a clear plastic case. After being satisfied he had what he came for, Mr. Takata reached into his briefcase and withdrew two flash drives.

Although George knew he had the diamond, he never opened the box and examined it. George was more than curious and wanted to check the cut and clarity of the diamond. "May I?"

Mr. Takata showed George the stone.

George was enamored. "So, this is it. The Ichiro diamond."

"Yes."

"If I understand the process correctly, they put Masato's ashes through a process that turned his remains into a diamond."

"Yes. Some call it preserving one's legacy. It is called an Eterneva Diamond."

"How does it work?"

"It is a six-part process. Beginning with the carbon purification of ashes, then a rough diamond is cultivated, cut, polished, engraved, and then finally set into a unique setting to be made into a family heirloom."

George looked at the fine detail of the diamond using a jeweler's loupe to magnify the engraving. "It even has his epitaph engraved on it."

"Yes, they use a fine laser to personally engrave the girdle of the diamond."

Mr. Takata held out one of the flash drives toward George. That was George's cue to return the diamond to Takata and in exchange, George took the flash drive and attached it to his computer.

Mr. Takata went on with the business at hand. "It's the list of new accounts and matching shipping labels. I'll be taking the diamond to the site myself."

George pulled up a shipping manifest and hit the icon for PRINT.

"I'll be sure the package gets delivered."

A customs manifest began to print out. The first company listed was, MayCo Construction, followed by Sunshine Travel, then Madeleine's Market.

CHAPTER 11

It was late in the day when Kyle approached his house, pulled up into the driveway, and turned off the engine. Kyle and Aiko sat there momentarily in silence. Neither one knew what to say that hadn't already been said. Kyle knew Aiko was a woman of few words. He also understood saying too much had the opposite effect on her, so he let the silence between them be the negotiator.

Kyle's cell phone rang, and the display read: P Dalton.

Kyle answered. "Yes, Sir."

As close as Aiko was she couldn't quite make out what the President was saying on the other end of the phone.

"Yes, Sir. I understand." Kyle hung up the phone.

Aiko couldn't wait for Kyle to tell her. "Oksana?"

"Nothing."

Aiko began to break down, she took a breath, then regained her composure. "I do not understand. No ransom demand, nothing? We know Oksana and Jillian can be tracked. How can there be nothing?"

Aiko's mind began to wander like that of a parent's when thinking of a lost child and not knowing. Kyle took Aiko's hand.

Kyle did his best to reassure her. "I will find her."

"How? We have nothing to go on."

Kyle showed Aiko the damaged ID badge he took off their assailant.

It read, MayCo Construction.

CHAPTER 12

Oksana woke up on a living room couch to see Jillian across from her, up leaning up against the kitchen counter. Jillian was still wearing the sweats their captors had given her. She was making something to eat in the small kitchen. Oksana realized she too was now wearing a set of sweats. She looked around and noticed there were no windows in what appeared to be a small apartment that was about 8 feet across and 40 feet long. All that she could hear was a small fan running from the air system.

"Where are we?" Oksana asked.

Jillian turned around. "I have no idea where we are or what time it is. All I know is we haven't eaten in a while, so I was trying to put something together."

Oksana stood, and as she walked over to the front door she adjusted the drawstring on her waistband. She tried the door. It was locked. Jillian had finished making the meal and set out the plates. Oksana joined Jillian at the small table set for two located just beyond the edge of the couch.

Jillian handed Oksana a small damp cloth. "Wipe your face and hands really good. As it turns out, enough of that cocaine powder must have gotten into your system and jacked you up. I tried to wipe off most of while you were sleeping but I didn't want to wake you."

Oksana cleaned up and started to snack. "My whole body feels tired. I just remember it feeling like bugs were on me and someone was touching me, like a ghost had its hand over my face. I could feel its fingertips going through my skin touching my skull."

"You must have inhaled more than I thought. Your body must have put out a lot of energy until you finally came down. How did you come into contact with it?"

"I fell into those boards you make the walls out of and got covered in white dust. I think it's called drywall. Except this drywall had a yellow cord running through it."

"They must be using the drywall to move the drugs."

"I think I still feel sick. Like the room is moving."

"It's not just you, I feel it too. I think we might be on the water, like in a houseboat or something."

"No really, I think I'm going to be sick."

Oksana ran to the back of the unit and threw up in the bathroom. After cleaning up she came back to the kitchen area.

Jillian took Oksana in her arms and hugged her. "Maybe it's the cocaine wearing off and you're feeling a bit claustrophobic in this small house?"

Jillian could tell that Oksana was still not herself. Oksana began to breathe a little deeper.

Jillian helped Oksana to the table. "Let me get you some water."

Oksana looked around her and could see the walls coming in all around her. As Jillian turned around to give Oksana the glass of water, she watched as Oksana jumped from the table, and go into a fight or flight mode. The small panic attack had turned into rage and she grabbed a nearby lamp, pulled off the shade, and used the base to try to break into the wall to make a window.

White dust began to fill the air and after a couple of heavy blows, Oksana struck something solid that sounded like a low deep bong. Oksana felt the lamp strike the metallic surface and reverberate up into her hands. She stopped chopping at the wall, looked oddly at the base of the lamp, and then at Jillian.

Jillian saw Oksana's face covered in white. "Oksana! Don't breathe."

Jillian grabbed the washcloth and quickly wiped Oksana's face. She handed the washcloth to Oksana and instructed her to blow her nose into it. Oksana did as she was instructed and then was finally able to take a breath.

Oksana saw a bit of white dust hovering in the air. "What is it?"

Jillian pointed out a hole in the wall. "Look."

Behind the drywall was a corrugated metal wall. Running inside the drywall was a yellow cord.

The handle to the unit's front door began to rattle.

Oksana's panic attack now felt like paranoia and immediately got her amped up again. "Someone's coming." Oksana grabbed the base of the lamp and got behind the door. The door opened.

Milo walked in and saw Jillian sitting at the table. "Where's the girl?"

Oksana quietly stepped out from behind the door and whacked Milo across the back of his neck with the lamp base. He dropped to his knees in pain.

Oksana ran out the door and quickly came to a stark reality. It was dawn and they were not in a boathouse but on a cargo ship, far out at sea.

Javier grabbed Oksana and took the lamp away from her and tossed it into a nearby empty trash barrel. Oksana turned around and she saw the small apartment they were held captive in was set up inside a 40-foot shipping container.

Inside the unit, Milo had made it to his feet and had Jillian at bay as Javier brought Oksana back into the isolated apartment. Jillian took Oksana in her arms.

Mr. Takata walked into the unit and saw the damage Oksana had done to the wall and he pointed to the hole. "As you can see, this unit is lined with a drywall that contains a yellow cord. That is primer cord. It is connected to a trigger. If you continue to try to escape…"

Jillian got the gist and did not want to frighten Oksana any more than was necessary. "I understand."

Javier had a certain way of talking that made Jillian's skin crawl. "I don't think you do."

Takata separated Jillian from Oksana then passed Jillian off to Javier. Takata pushed Oksana in the direction of the couch. Her momentum took her into the couch and she felt it was best to just take a seat. As it struck her what Aiko had once taught her, if you want to live in the moment, sometimes you must choose to fight another day.

Takata felt he didn't have time to deal with any more interruptions and focused his disgust at Javier, "Do what you were paid to do. Handle them." Takata turned and left the unit.

Milo took a seat at the table. He looked at Oksana and realized that he was only about five years older than her. She was now the age his sister would have been. It hit him hard. He felt he was still paying for what happened to her, and somehow knew he always would. He saw that Oksana had caught him not staring at her but through her.

Milo regained his composure and felt the anger from having missed out on growing up with his sister and took it out on Oksana. "What the fuck are you looking at?"

Javier had been eyeing Jillian and knew if he was going to follow through with his desire of her, this was going to have to be the time. As he stood in front of her, he grabbed Jillian by the waistband of her sweats and pulled them out enough to get a glance down the front of her. Jillian grabbed Javier's wrist to keep him from pulling any further.

Jillian reiterated, "I told you, I understand."

"And I'm telling you, no one is coming for you."

Javier pushed their hands down inside Jillian's sweats together as lovers might do to please each other but Jillian's body was far from willing. Jillian turned her body, so Oksana could not see what he was trying to do to her. Javier slipped in behind Jillian and pressed up against her.

Jillian could hear the vile tone in Javier's voice. "You and I are about to come to an even better understanding."

Javier used his body to push Jillian toward the bedroom. At the doorway, Jillian had to let go of Javier's hand to use both her hands to grab onto the door frame to keep herself from being forced into the bedroom.

Javier made his point, "Are you willing to die for your cause?"

"And what is your cause?"

"The ol' mighty dollar is my cause. It has a way of finding out what morals you're willing to comfortably live without."

Jillian still had tension in her arms. She felt Javier grab her between the legs. "Resist, and the girl will be next. And her, I'll do for free. That I will leave up to your morals."

Jillian's arms began to weaken, Javier thrust his hips and pushed Jillian into the bedroom. Jillian had to believe she would get her chance, but it would not happen if she was dead. Although her mind was resisting, she had to believe he would go after Oksana if she did not give herself to this animal.

Jillian turned to her captor. "Give me your word you will not touch Oksana."

Javier leaned in close to Jillian's neck and could smell the fear on her warm skin. "My momma told me not to make promises I can't keep. I guess it's going to depend on how ingratiating you are willing to be."

She thought one bit of salvation she might have was that she did not have to look at this man when he took her pride from her. With no windows in the room, she figured the darkness would be the one saving grace, so she reached over and turned off the light.

Javier wasn't having it. He wasn't going to miss a single thing about this. He slapped Jillian across the side of the face and she fell back onto the bed. He then reached over and turned the light back on.

Oksana could hear a slap from Jillian to Javier's face, followed by an even louder and harder slap to Jillian's face from Javier.

Milo looked at Oksana. She could sense that the torturous sounds coming from the next room were not in the plans that he agreed to when he signed on for this job. There was nothing he could do, the man in the other room was his father.

Oksana began to cry for Jillian's suffering.

The sounds of the shipping container at sea drowned out any and all sounds coming from inside the apartment container, including Jillian's screams.

Off in the distance were two tropical islands near one another. They were isolated and appeared to be the end of a larger chain that was a few miles beyond.

CHAPTER 13

On one of the walls inside Sunshine Travel was an image of a different set of islands, Hawaii. The picture was an enticement for vacationers to want to travel off on an exotic vacation.

The travel agent behind the desk was named Savannah. She had a postcard from Savannah Georgia with quotes drawn on it in pink highlighter, accentuating "Savannah" propped up on the front of her desk standing in for her nameplate. She was in the middle of handling her opening duties as the UPS driver entered with a package for her to sign for.

"Why, hello, Randy. Always nice to see you."

"Savannah."

"Looks like business is picking up. I've been delivering a lot more packages lately." Randy made his play. "You just might need a vacation yourself. Where would you like to take me?"

Savannah always liked Randy's playful charm. "How about you look over a few of these brochures and I'll get an outgoing package ready for you."

Randy, who had been holding back the package to keep the conversation going, handed it over to Savannah. After signing, Savannah checked the return label. The label read, MayCo Construction.

"I'll be right back."

In the back room, Savannah opened the medium-sized box and removed some of the packing peanuts to make space for her item. She removed a small box from a safe and added it to the original package. She threw back in as much of the packing peanuts as it would hold and resealed the box. She then added the travel agency's return label over the old label and added a new destination label.

The label read, Madeleine's Market.

CHAPTER 14

Kyle and Aiko were walking along the sidewalk just up the street from Madeleine's Market. Kyle knew he couldn't keep anything from Aiko too long. "I talked with Dalton this morning."

"It has been days since we have heard anything, and you are just telling me this now?"

"I didn't want you to get your hopes up. It looks like he might have a lead on their location based on a faint ping they got. I'm waiting to hear back from Dalton. He's waiting to hear back from Casey. If it pans out, we'll join Casey to investigate the location."

"I hate the waiting."

Kyle only brought it up now as a distraction. He was not aware if Aiko knew how close they were to where they first met. A few blocks over would have them in the Pearl District. Everything was rushing back to Kyle. The shootout in the warehouse that took his brother's life. The ricochet from his gun that hit Aiko.

"What is it, Kyle?" Aiko asked.

Aiko must have caught him in a daze.

"Nothing. Just thinking about you."

"Am I nothing to you?"

Kyle understood Aiko's attempt at a joke. "I am so grateful to have met you and at times it brings me back to what has happened to us and where we are now."

"In what way?"

"My bullet almost took your life."

"Kyle, your bullet saved my life."

Kyle stopped walking. Aiko took a step past Kyle and turned back toward him. "Were we in the wrong place at the wrong time or the right place? If your bullet had missed, where would we be right now? Not here. Not together."

Kyle leaned down and kissed Aiko.

"I do not harbor regrets," Aiko continued. "We may have been through very tough times but if I had the choice, I would rather be here than still under the Masato name. That world is no longer my world. You and Oksana are my world now."

Kyle had no words and loved everything Aiko just said. Kyle took Aiko's hand, kissed the back of it, and with a little pirouette spun Aiko around. They continued their walk, in silence, but their hearts spoke volumes.

Kyle and Aiko approached the market. There were a few small groups of local college kids just milling around outside the market. The store had a couple of wooden picnic tables along the sunny side of the market, as did a lot of the eateries in the area for guests. Half the students chilled as the other half seemed to be a little antsy.

A UPS truck pulled up around the corner on the other side of the store to be close to the back door of the market. The UPS driver was greeted by the stock boy of the market, who took a medium-sized box.

Kyle noticed the chatter from the crowd outside the market seemed to have perked up. He opened the door for Aiko, she took the lead, and he followed her in.

Kyle exchanged a wave and a hello to the girl behind the counter. "Hello, Mads."

"Hello, officer Morrell. How are you today?"

"We're good, thank you."

Kyle and Aiko lingered in the store at the fresh vegetable section to find what he and Aiko wanted to make for dinner. Kyle got a glimpse outside at the stirring crowd as one of them came into the store and headed to the back of the market, followed by another.

Kyle and Aiko approached Madeleine at the register with a small basket of greens along with fresh chicken to make up a tasty stir-fry. Kyle looked out at the crowd and asked Madeleine, "Is everything okay?"

"Yeah, they're harmless. It's my regular Saturday lunch crowd. They're always a bit jumpy. Maybe they know you're a cop and it's got them amped up."

Kyle paid for the groceries and he and Aiko left the store.

As Kyle and Aiko left the market, a couple of the college kids entered and headed directly to the back of the store.

Kyle walked up the street with Aiko and saw two more college students heading their way. One of the students passed a couple of $20 bills to the other, who then added two of his own twenties to the pot. As the students passed Kyle, he watched as one of the students folded the bills together and put the cash into a small Manila envelope.

Back in the market, a college student was holding a soft drink in one hand as he opened the door to the cooler, slipped a small Manila envelope in a thin slot in the back behind the drinks, and then grabbed a second drink.

The student moved a couple of doors down to where the fresh, premade sandwiches were on display. All the rows in the display were filled with a variety of hoagie type sandwiches. The row on the left side of the shelf was empty. The student grabbed one prepared sandwich and a moment later, a freshly wrapped sandwich was loaded from the back of the cooler and slid down the empty shelf on the left. The student added that sandwich to the rest of his selected items and headed to the cashier.

Madeleine rang up the student, who then left the store, as two more entered. As the young college student walked out of the market he took a seat at one of the nearby picnic tables. He handed a girl one of the sandwiches. The girl unwrapped her sandwich, opened her soda, and took a glancing look around as she took a sip of her drink. Getting the sense everything was cool, she nodded. The boyfriend unwrapped his sandwich. He lifted the top layer off bread of his sandwich, removed a long thin bag filled with cocaine, and slipped it into his jacket pocket.

Kyle and Aiko had doubled back and had been observing this ritual for some time. Two go in, another two exit like kids leaving a candy store.

*****

Inside the market storage room, one of the walls was designed for loading the cooler from the back. The stock boy removed a small manila envelope from a drop box that was attached for payments located by the back of the cooler, behind the sodas. He turned to drop the money into a box in exchange for one of the special hoagies, when he saw a shadow on the ground. Kyle's shadow.

The stock boy looked up and saw both Kyle and Aiko. "This is for deliveries only."

Kyle let the stock boy know he wasn't lost. "This is a delivery. I'd like to deliver you and your sandwiches to the police station."

The stock boy panicked and began grabbing anything he could to throw at Kyle and Aiko. First, it was quarts of milk, then yogurt, and then he grabbed a can of soda. He judged the weight of the can then hurled it at Kyle. Then another.

As Kyle was ducking the first can he got hit on the side of his head by the second. Kyle reacted by spinning out of the way and Aiko stepped in.

The stock boy hurled a can of Coke at Aiko. She didn't flinch and caught it cleanly.

The stock boy wasn't ready for that. "Ah, hell no."

From outside the market came the stock boy having been tossed out onto his ass by Aiko. His momentum sent him hurling hard into the side of a parked car. He sat there in a daze.

Kyle and Aiko walked out of the back of the market. Kyle was covered in milk and yogurt and was rubbing the side of his head.

Aiko turned to Kyle, "Are you alright?"

Kyle took a look at himself and couldn't help but take the sarcasm. "Just getting my daily dose of calcium handed to me."

All Aiko had to show for the fight was a little spot of milk on her cheek that Kyle reached over and wiped away.

Aiko assessed the stock boy and saw that he was no real threat, then turned to see Kyle trying to wipe away a clump of yogurt. "Now what?"

Kyle raised his left hand and showed the return label he had removed from the box that was in the storeroom of the market to Aiko.

Aiko was thinking from her conversation with Kyle earlier, that they had a possible lead to Oksana's location. She didn't want anything more to do with this stock boy and his little franchise. "We do not have time to follow this case. We need to focus on getting Oksana."

Kyle held up his right hand with another return label and jingled the first label in the other. "And this label was under this label."

Aiko took a closer look at the second label. The label read, MayCo Construction.

Kyle took out his cell phone and called Dalton. "Sir, we have a lead." After a moment, "Yes, we can meet you at Air Force One, but first we are going to need some time to get cleaned up." After another short pause, "Yes, seven would be fine, Sir. We look forward to it." Kyle hung up the phone.

"What did he say?"

"It looks like we are having dinner with the President."

CHAPTER 15

Kyle was in the bathroom wearing only a towel just after he finished his shower. He wiped away the steam from the mirror. Looking at his reflection, he saw a scar on his shoulder that, to this day is still a haunting memory that will never go away, but he is okay with that. It's a reminder of the strength he and Aiko have together. The scar was actually made up of a series of repeated lashings he had to endure while he stayed silent as not to break and give away his affection for Aiko. Kyle felt if they broke him, and they killed Aiko, he would have rather they had finished the job. The scars led up and over his shoulder blade and continued down through the middle of his back.

A memory of strength over weakness, terms Aiko used to describe one's empowerment to overcome and survive. Along his neck was another reminder left behind from the noose that seemed to want to slowly take his life, rather than be efficient and put him out of his misery. Kyle touched the side of his neck and felt the memory travel all the way to the bottom of his feet. A phantom sensation from standing barefoot on the ends of short bamboo poles as his life was being drawn from him with each strike of the whip.

Aiko came in behind him also wearing just a towel. Aiko traced her fingers down his back over his scars, soothing his thoughts.

Kyle's recollection of the first time Aiko touched him after that painful memory was burned into him and came rushing back. "I've been thinking about what you did." Their eyes connected in the mirror. "In front of everyone, you gave yourself to us, by saving my life."

Aiko lowered her head. Kyle turned to face Aiko. "I could not let them kill you because of me."

"It was more than that. You showed them you were not like them. You showed them the woman you have become."

"I will always be a Masato. That I cannot change. My family name is without honor."

Kyle moved in behind Aiko and slid down her towel to look at the scars she took to save him. They were like claw marks over the black and white tattoo that covered her back from her shoulders to the small of her back.

Kyle could still feel the way Aiko's body flinched from each strike of the whip when she had used her body to support him and save his life. His fingers tenderly floated across the embedded memory in her skin that will forever show her courage and the love she showed for him.

Kyle continued to run his fingers gently down Aiko's back. "Family does not do this."

Kyle and Aiko made eye contact in the mirror once more.

"Oksana and I are your family now."

"What I have been through, I do not deserve you."

Kyle maneuvered Aiko between him and the counter so they both faced the mirror. He reached around Aiko's slender body and placed his hand inside Aiko's towel and rested his hand on her lower abdomen. "And yet what has brought us together has given both of us a second chance." Kyle kissed the back of Aiko's neck as he hugged her from behind. "I honor you."

"You can honor me by letting me go from your debt."

"Aiko, that is what I want you to understand. I never considered you in any debt of service to me or us. I love you just for you."

Aiko turned around and let her towel fall to the ground. "Then I honor you as well."

Aiko ran her hands down over Kyle's chest and when she got to his towel, she undid the tension, and it dropped to the floor next to hers. Kyle picked her up and she wrapped her legs around his waist as his arms held her body close to his. He carried her over to the bed, never taking his eyes away from her gaze. As they passed by the light switch, Aiko reached out and switched the light off.

The glow of the full moon passed through the Venetian blinds that had remained open just enough, and at the right angle to allow the light to set the room in a blue-gray tone. The white down comforter on the bed was warm and soft to the touch on Aiko's back as Kyle laid her gently down.

The contours of Aiko's body were now highlighted from the parallel beams of light through the blinds that now formed an illusion like an ever-flowing symphonic chart rolling across her. As she moved, so did the artistry that was her beauty. Kyle leaned in and kissed her between her breasts. He could feel her lungs fill with air as she gasped deeply. The passion he felt was so exotic from her skin that was beyond the softness he sensed on his lips.

Aiko wrapped her arms around Kyle as his kisses moved upward to her mouth. She wrapped one leg around him to hold him there. Kyle ran his hand through Aiko's wet hair, cradled the back of her head, and spoke from his heart as he kissed her. Even without words, Aiko understood every loving thought he felt for her.

Kyle raised himself up to his knees as he knelt between her legs. He looked at her like he had never been in love before, not until he met her. This was different, and he wanted to show her what she truly meant to him with every kiss, touch of his hand, and with every promise his eyes made to her. The strands of light were intoxicating as they only accentuated her natural beauty.

He leaned in once more and kissed her between her neck and shoulder.

Aiko put her hand on the back of his head and gripped a handful of his hair. She kissed his neck. Kyle caressed her breast cupping her tenderly and Aiko replied by letting Kyle feel her teeth gently bite into his shoulder. Neither one was in control. Time was irrelevant.

Kyle felt Aiko's skin already warm getting warmer with each kiss. He could feel Aiko's hand on the back of his head pressing down. He began to follow her desire. He kissed her tummy below her belly button with his arms stretched out caressing her skin, running his hands up to cup her supple breasts. He felt Aiko wrap both her legs around his shoulders and held him there as her body arched. The beams of moonlight swelled like waves across her body just like the sensation she felt transcending through her.

Kyle brought down one hand and cupped behind Aiko's lower back and lifted Aiko, sliding her further up onto the bed. There was no more waiting. Their bodies entwined and were as one. The beams of moonlight rolled over them as rhythmically as the tide is controlled by the moon. Love was the seventh wave.

CHAPTER 16

In the darkness of the shipping container apartment, only a few small indicator lights could be seen from the clock on the microwave. The unit's interior fluorescent lights began to flicker on. One of the two main lights were out so the second tube had a hard time coming on and only flickered to half its brightness.

Jillian had already awakened and was lying in bed. Oksana woke up to the sound of the door being opened. She could not only hear the ship's horn sounding, she could feel the vibrations emanating from its low tone travel through the ship.

Oksana turned to Jillian. "Where are we?"

The answer did not come from Jillian but from Mr. Takata, "NuFa 23."

Jillian and Oksana turned to see Takata who was standing in the frame of the bedroom door. With what little light there was in the room, Takata could see Jillian's face. Jillian lowered her head in shame which told Takata that Javier had done more than just backhand her.

"I didn't tell him to do that."

Jillian looked up, "And that makes it alright?"

"We will be departing in five minutes." Takata turned out of the doorway.

Oksana had to ask, "What's a NuFa?"

*****

As Takata left, he left the doors of the unit open. Oksana helped Jillian to her feet as her body was still sore from the abuse she had to endure from that rat bastard, Javier. They made their way over to the door. The light from the sun was even more harsh for Jillian because of the sensitivity of the direct sunlight to her right eye. Her vision blurred as her eye began to water from the trauma of Javier's backhand across her face. The solid impact of the blow had also given her a ringing in her ears that was turned up a notch from the brightness of the sun. Once Jillian's eyes were able to adjust, they worked their way over close to the edge of the ship and saw there was a small barge alongside the ship.

The fresh sea air was the only good thing that seemed to connect with Jillian's senses. Having grown up in Connecticut, it reminded her of home and her family weekend outings to the coast except that the air here was more warm and humid, tropical. The sun was high, and the horizon seemed to go on forever. She saw one of the deck hands was drinking a Kalik beer and the other had a parrot on his shoulder. It was green with blue feathers on the end of its wings. The chest was red, and the head had a white crown. She had seen this bird before and had quenched her thirst on Kalik beer on her college senior trip. She knew they had to be somewhere in the Bahamas.

The container ship had a large cargo crane that was hovering over the container that was Jillian's and Oksana's apartment. The workers had finished attaching the thick cables to the corners of the container as another worker removed the power coupling and water lines from the unit.

Mr. Takata motioned to Jillian and Oksana, "I'm going to have to ask you to head back inside now."

As Jillian and Oksana entered the container, a woman holding Mr. Takata's briefcase handed it to him and he too entered the container. He locked the door and took a seat at the table.

The arm of the crane began to slowly move and caused the cables on the container to go taut.

Jillian and Oksana were standing in the beams of light from the emergency lighting system that had kicked on.

"You might want to take a seat," Takata urged.

The container began to move, and Jillian and Oksana quickly took a seat next to each other on the couch.

Jillian asked, "Where are you taking us? What is NuFa 23?"

"NuFa 23 is an abandoned nuclear fallout shelter that for all intents and purposes, no longer exists. An off the books island paradise from your government. An island paradise that holds a secret that would fulfill most dreams."

The container landed with a hard jolt as it was transferred to a tug-barge that had been modified with a large storage hold and room on deck for a single 40-foot shipping container.

Mr. Takata let the echo dissipate before reiterating his point, "Welcome to NuFa 23; your new home."

From the side of the container ship, the arm of the crane rose back onto the ship for the last time, having previously unloaded pallets of food, supplies, and 55-gallon drums full of fuel. The roar of the tug's engines propelled the ship's cargo toward the small lavishly thick jungle island that was covered with tropical foliage and unknown dangers.

*****

The multiple layers of jungle growth were plentiful with life on the island that was about the size of a major university. The sounds of the waves crashing on the rocks faded the deeper into the jungle you went, and those sounds were replaced by the sounds of the jungle coming alive with songs from a whole host of exotic birds.

A small bird was on the ground having fallen from its protective nest. A feral raccoon was gently nudging the small bird. About 25 feet behind the raccoon was a tiger. The tiger saw its opportunity for a meal, crouched, and was getting ready to pounce.

Just as the tiger began rushing its prey, its feet were slipping on the old foliage that covered the jungle floor and alerted the raccoon of the danger. The raccoon screamed and never looked back as it ran for its life.

The raccoon had cleared the space where the tiger landed with a thud and came to a sliding stop in the dirt near the little bird.

The tiger was not moving. There was a tranquilizer dart sticking out from its hindquarters. The shooter dressed in jungle camouflage gear stepped into the clearing holding a tranquilizer rifle. He removed his hat to reveal it was Zen.

Birgitta was behind Zen, and she signaled to her team that was following them to net the large cat. As she walked up alongside Zen and slung her rifle over her left shoulder, she put her right arm around Zen and pressed her fit twenty-something body into his. She knew very well what she was doing as she teased him by rubbing her breast up against him.

"Nice shot, Zen. You're quite the young man."

Zen thought of himself as a man but his awareness of how shy he was around Birgitta made it hard for the seventeen-year-old to express himself as a man. Zen barely got the words out. "Thank you, Birgitta."

Birgitta smiled at Zen as she rubbed her hand gently down his back. She could feel how tight his body was from all the martial arts training he had been through in the last couple of years.

"Let's get this lovely specimen back to the lab and show Kamiko what a fine marksman you are, and the man you are becoming."

Birgitta turned and walked toward the truck. Zen took a moment to watch Birgitta walk away. He could feel his breathing coming back to normal, but his heart was still a flutter as he could still smell Birgitta's perfume lingering on and around him.

Birgitta pressed the activation button on her walkie-talkie. "We have the prize."

Birgitta glanced back and caught Zen looking at her in a slight trance, just as she wanted. She was charming, and he was charmed.

A truck drove up into the clearing with a large steel cage on the back of its flatbed. As the workers carried the sedated beast over to the truck in the cargo net and loaded it in, Birgitta looked off into the distance and saw the barge with the container aboard getting closer to the island.

*****

The pilot of the barge had a setting that was leading the ship directly toward a large rock wall covered in roots and foliage on the north end of the island. As the barge approached, the rock wall was actually a giant façade. A fortified metal mesh weaved with artificial foliage made up of ivy, palm, and tree roots. On approach, the retractable arms opened the mesh to allow the barge to enter the cave-like opening.

*****

The inside of the reconfigured fallout shelter was a fully functional landing pier. As the barge came to a full stop, the dock workers took over securing the ship.

The door to the container apartment opened. Mr. Takata exited with his briefcase in hand and quickly headed for the dock. Jillian and Oksana followed but were a bit more cautious as they took in their new surroundings. Large lights hung from the cave's ceiling. They watched as the cave's opening closed behind them. Rough rock formations from the water's edge turned into man-made steps which led up to the far end of the dock.

The workers set a large plank in place to allow Mr. Takata to exit from the barge to the dock. As Mr. Takata reached the dock, an electric golf cart approached, and he took a seat. He looked back and saw that Oksana had stopped to watch two men who were sitting on 5-gallon buckets, fishing off the end of the pier. Takata motioned to Jillian, who in turn tapped Oksana on the shoulder to get her attention, to get a move on to catch up to Takata as he was already taking a seat on the golf cart.

As the cart pulled away from the dock, a large cargo arm was maneuvering to unload the apartment container to get to the cargo hold below. The golf cart passed a large stack of empty 55-gallon drums. The golf cart turned and headed down a long cement sewer-like tube hallway which had a few more passages forking off it.

Oksana tugged on Jillian's sleeve. "This is like Skylab but underground."

The passages were 20 feet around with wide flat bottoms and recessed lighting, and were part of the fully functional, self-contained, working environment known as NuFa 23.

From one of the side tunnels, Birgitta and her team had the tiger in its cage and were delivering it to the dock to have the exotic cat loaded onto the barge. As they made the turn at the fork, Birgitta and her team saw the golf cart with Jillian and Oksana pass by and disappear off into the distance. Birgitta once again felt betrayed. The First Lady here on the island? Why hadn't she been informed? It made her wonder what else was being kept from her.

Oksana was worried what Jillian was going to say but had to make sure what she heard was correct. "What did he mean by this is going to be our new home? Isn't anyone coming for us?"

Jillian didn't know what to say and saying nothing made it worse.

CHAPTER 17

Outside the White House, a car pulled up to a security gate. One of the Marine guards approached the car. The driver's window was already down, and Kyle handed the Marine Sergeant his and Aiko's passports.

"We're here by the request of the President."

The Marine checked their passports against his log sheet. "Thank you, Mr. Morrell. The President has been expecting you. Welcome to the White House."

The secretary knocked on the outer door of the Oval Office, opened it, and showed Kyle and Aiko into the Oval Office.

Pres. Dalton greeted them and led them to the settee area. "Welcome to the White House. Can I get you anything to drink before dinner?" Dalton had thought of Aiko and her just finding out she was pregnant. "Water perhaps?"

Kyle and Aiko both declined.

Dalton gestured to the Secret Service agent, "Thank you. That will be all."

The agent took a post just outside the door.

Dalton gestured to the sofa, "Please, have a seat."

Kyle and Aiko sat on one of the two matching sofas and Dalton sat opposite them.

Kyle felt out of place, yet really didn't mind. "I thought Air Force One was intimidating."

Dalton tried to make them feel at ease, "First, I want to thank you for understanding why I had to return to Washington. The details of which I have to keep secret, just like our off-book rescue operation to get my wife back, and of course to rescue Oksana as well. And how we go about doing that is already underway. That is why I requested you here today."

Aiko was impressed and impatient. "If you have a plan, then you must know where they are?"

Before Dalton could answer, there was a knock at the door.

Dalton took the distraction as a way to keep everyone calm, "Enter."

Secret Service agent Malone entered. "Sir, dinner is ready."

"Thank you, Agent Malone." Dalton put out his hand to help Aiko off the couch, "I asked the chef to make a special meal in your honor Aiko."

Aiko did not like the special attention, "Thank you, but you did not have to do that just for me."

"To be honest, I happen to be a fan of yakitori."

Kyle replied, "I know that one. Barbequed chicken on a stick."

Aiko shook her head thinking, "Gaijin."

Agent Malone led the group to the blue room just down the hall.

"I had the staff set us up in here for dinner. It's a little less formal and has a nice view of the South Lawn.

Aiko saw that not only had they made yakitori as part of the dinner, but they had also prepared the fried rice dish, chehan. Next to that was a plate of yakisoba noodles with pork and chicken. But what really got her attention was the bowl of nikujaga, a beef stew dish with potato in a sweet soy broth.

Aiko looked at Kyle and Kyle knew the jig was up.

Kyle confessed, "I got a call from the White House chef and he asked, what dishes were your favorite?" Kyle hesitated, "Did I get it right?"

Aiko looked over the table once more, "Yes, Kyle-san. You got it right."

The President pulled out a seat for Aiko at the small table. Kyle sat next to her and Dalton across from them. After their meal, agent Malone handed the president a note, then left.

Kyle had to know, "Did you receive a ransom note? What do they want?"

Dalton was being cautious. He waited until Malone had closed the door. "Recently we received a very weak signal just long enough to give a location."

Aiko felt he knew more than he was sharing so she asked her question another way, more direct. "Where are they?"

"The signal originated near a series of small islands near an abandoned military base. Before we go any further, we're going to need to confirm the location without drawing any attention from anyone, especially the media. As far as anyone knows, Jillian is still on vacation with friends on the West Coast."

Kyle asked Aiko's next question. "Was there just one signal? Anything about Oksana?"

"That is where you come in. I am re-tasking you, Aiko, and our team led by Casey, to confirm the signal and the whereabouts of Jillian and Oksana."

Kyle again spoke for himself and Aiko. "When do we leave?"

"I have my man Casey and his team standing by with a jet waiting for you and Aiko as we speak."

Everyone stood.

"Remember, for security reasons, no one can know where you're going."

Aiko let Dalton know her priorities. "The only person who concerns me right now is Oksana."

CHAPTER 18

Under the canopy of the jungle of NuFa 23 was a camouflaged back entrance that led into the reconfigured nuclear fallout shelter. The door opened, a worker walked out carrying a box of kitchen scraps, mainly made up of vegetables, and tossed the contents of the box onto a compost pile. The worker turned to head back into the shelter when he saw a leopard watching him from near the corner of the building. The worker slowly set the empty box down and took a slow side step toward the back entrance. The leopard countered by taking a couple of steps in his direction. The frightened man stopped.

The 200-pound Persian leopard had been brought to the island for breeding. It was Kamiko's idea that her clients were willing to pay top dollar for an exotic wild animal, so she would let the beast wander freely to make sure they wouldn't become too domesticated. Although they were used to being in the company of man, the worker knew there was no chance he could run and not be chased, so he remained as still as he possibly could. There was a small vent coming off the side of the building with a light, white smoke coming from it, with an aroma of cooked meat from the kitchen grill. The worker was frightened that the leopard might mistake the scent in the air as coming from him and cause the carnivorous animal to want to partake in his flesh as his afternoon snack. That's when the leopard began to slowly take another step forward. The worker could feel his leg shaking as he took a step back, then as the leopard proceeded to take one slow precise step after another, the worker countered with the same number of steps to keep his distance. The man found himself getting closer to the compost pile and further away from the door. The cat was now closer to the entrance to NuFa than to the worker. Then the unthinkable happened, the hungry leopard paused, lifted his nose into the air and followed the aroma coming from inside. Then it turned its attention to the open door and walked into the facility. The terror-stricken man knew he had to warn his coworkers. In what he thought was a moment of temporary insanity, he overcame his fear and ran back in the door after the elusive animal.

*****

Inside one of the many rooms in the fallout shelter, Kamiko had a common wall in her quarters removed. This opened her room to the adjoining door to make her unit twice as large. Plus, hers was the only room to have a bay window in it that faced the ocean.

Kamiko was at her desk on the phone, "Are we compromised?" Kamiko listened intently to the other end of the conversation. "I will take care of my end of the deal." Kamiko listened. "This would give you complete anonymity as long as you hold up your end of the deal."

In the oval office Pres. Dalton was on a secured cell phone, "Oksana was not part of the deal."

Kamiko was holding a jewel case containing a CD in her other hand and was fanning herself with it as she talked to Dalton. "I know it was you who ordered the raid on my business in Portland. My man took the cell phones off those two FBI agents and one of their last calls was from you."

There was a long silence as Dalton's mind quickly went over the events that led up to the loss of two of his best agents. He opened a desk drawer and saw an old file among many. He didn't have to open it to know its contents. He had assigned agents Cabral and Caceres to see if they could track down his silent partner's location and retrieve a certain CD. The lead had not taken them to Kamiko but to her brother's end of the operation in Portland, Oregon. The agents were on stakeout just up the street from the Japanese Garden when they were ambushed by Kamiko's assassin, Karl Bogdanoff. He was sent there to keep an eye on not only Kamiko's interest in the family business and to see if things were running smoothly, but also to confirm the rumors of her brother Ichiro's actions with their daughter were true.

The FBI once had a source inside the Masato's import-export business known as Red Sun Exports. The agent's last correspondence said she was trying to escape with the help of a friend, to have some collaborating evidence on how the girls were being kidnapped, enslaved, then sold on the black market.

Dalton thought he had what he needed to get out from under Kamiko until he got the report that the two girls that had escaped had been killed. Their bodies were discovered only after a car accident had given away their location. A BMW had crashed into a set of traffic barrels just off the highway, near a rest stop. Bogdanoff had been assigned by Hatashi, who was Masato's head of security, to locate, kill, and dispose of the bodies.

The report went on to say that the girls had been shot at point-blank range, with two shots to the chest and left in the traffic barrels filled with pool acid to get rid of any identification.

Before the bodies could completely dissolve, the crash exposing their fate had also left enough evidence for identification such as tattoo's, DNA, and dental records to conclude that one of the girls, in fact, was known to be the FBI's inside source.

Kamiko continued, "I also know you tried to send one of your teams to my compound in Niigata, but as you know they were too late. Do you know how I know this?"

Dalton had this nagging feeling, the feeling of always being a step behind. Dalton's mind whirled like one of the old-fashioned kaleidoscopes showing the man running on an endless loop, and just when you thought the man was going to get somewhere, that little hitch in the process had the man starting his run all over again.

Dalton had a four-man special ops team raid Kamiko's warehouse in Niigata just after the events that led to Kyle and Aiko's escape. Intel had shown them that Kamiko was on a quest to locate a rare stone known as the Monarch Moon. The team's assignment was to gather intel and acquire the stone before Kamiko, in order to have leverage to trade for the incriminating information that was burned into the CD.

As fate would have it, Kyle and Aiko's escape forced Kamiko's hand and caused her to move on, ahead of schedule. Before her untimely departure, Kamiko had assigned her accountant, Mr. Takata, to remove all the pertinent information from the computers before destroying them. Not only did Takata leave no trace, he also had shipped out all the artifacts to a temporary location, The George Anthony Studios, back in the states. When Dalton's team arrived, all they could do was report back, "We're too late."

Dalton closed the desk drawer and took a deep breath as he slowly rolled the stiffness out of his neck. He held back his displeasure at being manipulated this way by Kamiko as she continued turning the knife. "I am holding the CD they were after. The CD with my set of entry codes. The same CD that holds all the photos of you as Senator, in all your glory, strapped spread-eagled across a hotel bed." Kamiko paused so she knew she had Dalton's full attention, "I own you." Kamiko hung up the phone.

Dalton hung up on his end and dialed another number. The ringing stopped as the call went through. He only had one order, "Take her out."

CHAPTER 19

Kyle and Aiko met up with Casey at the shipyard.

Casey was on his cell phone, "Yes, Sir."

Aiko looked around at all the shipping containers. She thought as much as they all look the same, she noticed more and more detail. How the color schemes changed, some showed their age more than others, and then there were the numbers. It made her think about how many of these corrugated metal boxes at one time or another were used in human trafficking.

The more Aiko thought about it, she began to see the individuality of each container representing another life taken, sold, or killed. It began to overwhelm her as the more she looked around, the number of containers grew. When they drove into the shipyard, Aiko not only saw containers to be loaded onto ships standing by in the Willamette River but also multiple railroad tracks running north and south through the yard. Because of the size of it and the amount of non-stop rumbling from the coming and going of semis in and out of the yard, she got the feeling it was a major Northwest hub. It quickly became clear that what looked like a 1,000-piece puzzle was, in reality, a 10,000-piece puzzle with each container representing a piece and no picture on the box to cheat from. Then her heart sank. Aiko felt incomplete and her Oksana was the missing piece from her puzzle.

Kyle was looking at Aiko and got a sense of her loss from the pain she was holding back. He knew it was in her nature not to show pain but he himself understood the emptiness when the three of them were apart. Kyle stood behind Aiko and put his arms around her.

Aiko leaned back into Kyle and felt his strength. "She is out there, Kyle, and she's scared."

"I think you gave her your will and she knows that we will never stop looking for her, and that gives her hope."

Kyle heard Casey walking up behind them. Casey collected his thoughts as he hung up the cell phone.

"Is everything all right?" Kyle asked.

Aiko needed to know, "Do you have a location on Oksana?"

Casey let them in on what he knew. "Looks like we are closing in."

"Closing in, on what?" Kyle asked.

Casey's job was to keep his true assignment to himself. Dalton had promised Casey a posting in his cabinet once this mission was completed. Casey was the type of guy to always keep his options open. He knew the private sector was where the money was to be made.

Casey played it close to the vest. "I was given coordinates with a high probability that we now have the

First Lady's location narrowed down to a few square miles someplace in the Caicos Islands."

"Where is that exactly?" Aiko asked.

To Kyle, what sounded vague at first was becoming more like a high probability for success because of the open space and getting a good strong signal. A few square miles in the Caicos Islands didn't leave a very large grid to search. But why didn't Casey sound more positive in his information?

Kyle had thought Casey had been given the same need to know orders from the president. He knew he and Casey hadn't built up enough trust to be as mutually forthcoming with the tactical details of the assignment and it made him a bit apprehensive.

Even though Kyle knew exactly where it was, he reminded himself to be as cautious. "I believe it's about 350 miles east of Cuba in the Atlantic."

Casey got the point and acknowledged with a slight nod of the head. Casey understood that Kyle knew exactly where it was and that if they were going to have the best chance of rescuing the First Lady and Oksana, they were going to have to pool their resources, and that was going to have to start with trust.

CHAPTER 20

Although the walls of Kamiko's office within the fallout shelter were made of cement, she could hear a commotion out in the hallway and went to the door. Just as she opened the door, she saw the wild leopard, loose and slowly trotting past her door and down the hallway.

Kamiko stepped out into the hall as the worker who let the untamed beast in came running down the hall with a tranquilizer pistol. He was followed by two other workers with a net. Kamiko grabbed a tranquilizer pistol from the worker, took aim down the hall, and yelled in the direction of the leopard.

The leopard froze as Kamiko's scream echoed through the tubular chamber, disorienting the animal. The leopard turned in search of the source of the noise. As the large cat turned, it gave Kamiko a better target and she fired the tranquilizer. The dart hit the front shoulder of the wild intruder, causing the animal to flinch uncontrollably for a moment as it tried to shake off the source of the pain. The sedative took effect quickly and the leopard's legs gave way. The once proud animal rolled over and gave in to the sleep-inducing narcotic.

Two of Kamiko's guards approached. One of the guards had a knife pouch attached to his belt. Kamiko lifted the flap and slowly pulled one of the Kunai six-inch blades from the sheath. The worker that was responsible for letting the leopard into the facility started running down the hall in the opposite direction. Kamiko flipped the tactical knife around and caught the blade in her palm, quickly adjusted her grip, and hurled the knife. It struck the worker in the middle of his back plunging the blade in only inches from his heart. The man dropped to the floor in agony.

Kamiko's aim was off. The man lived. "Take him to Dr. Horst. If he lives, kill him."

The two men with the cargo net went to the aid of the man and put him on the net and started to drag him to the medical facility. As the injured man was being dragged by the guards, the guard whose knife Kamiko used, reached down and without mercy, retrieved his knife.

Kamiko had already made her way down the hall toward the sedated leopard. She removed the tranquilizer dart from the beautifully spotted animal and gently ran her fingers through the Persian leopard's soft fur coat.

"Not to worry. You will be headed to a fine home soon."

One of the dock workers approached and stood patiently until he had Kamiko's attention.

Kamiko stood. "Yes, what is it?"

The worker bowed, "Mr. Takata has arrived." The worker bowed once more then continued with his duties.

It was the news Kamiko had been waiting to hear. She headed down one of the main tunnels escorted by her two guards.

After a series of turns, they came to a room with a reinforced door. Alongside the door was a security pad that needed a key card to track all who entered and their dates and time of entry. Mr. Takata stood patiently outside the door waiting for Kamiko to arrive. As Kamiko approached, Mr. Takata swiped his security card across the pad. The buzzer sounded as the latch was released. One of the guards stepped forward and opened the door.

Jillian and Oksana were inside the 20 by 20 square foot cement vault. The room had been converted into a high-end holding cell complete with all the amenities, except a door handle on the inside. The interior walls had been softened and framed with drywall. Like the shipping container, the room was boxy, no windows, and the air was pumped in from a set of ducts from high above.

Kamiko's guard entered first taking up most of the doorway followed by Kamiko, Mr. Takata, and then the other guard.

Jillian stepped forward to confront Kamiko, but the guard put out his big paw and pressed it against Jillian's chest stopping her in her tracks. Then with little effort, he pushed her back into the middle of the room.

Kamiko let everyone know she was in charge. "Before you start trying to negotiate, you need to understand something, you're not being held for any ransom."

"Then why did you kidnap us?" Jillian asked.

"We were only tasked to acquire you. The girl is a bonus."

"I don't understand. Why are we here if not for ransom?"

"You are a distraction. While the White House staff is busy trying to keep your disappearance out of the news, no one will notice that it was your husband who sold you out. Your husband, the President of the United States, no longer needs you by his side. You were starting to make too many headlines with your little pet project and raising the focus on an enterprise that needs to stay as it has always been, under the radar."

Kamiko looked around Jillian at Oksana. "Now that he has what he needed from the girl, I guess he no longer needs her, as well."

Oksana showed her heart as she often does. "That's not true!"

Kamiko reached into Mr. Takata's satchel and pulled out a clear jewel case containing a CD. She waved it a bit for effect as she made her statement.

"I'm afraid it is. He seemed to be more concerned with a particular CD I have containing the future of his legacy."

Kamiko motioned to one of the guards who took Jillian by the arm and led her out of the room. Oksana stepped forward and the second guard showed his tranquilizer gun. Oksana stopped.

Oksana wasn't about to just stand by. "Where are you taking her?"

"To show her what this is all about." Kamiko took a few steps back and stood by the door. "And if you are thinking about trying to escape, these walls contain the same explosives as your container, so I would not try to press your luck a second time. It just takes a small amount of primer cord to blow a hole through a wall, so you can imagine if you happen to be in a room lined with it when it just so happened to go off."

Oksana looked around and quickly gauged the amount of explosive. She remembered seeing the yellow primer cord running through the drywall as the construction workers were digging her out after her fall. She could visualize the amount primer cord that was crisscrossing throughout the walls of her cell.

As Kamiko left Oksana to ponder the explosion that would implode the room, the walls of the room all of a sudden seemed to be getting smaller and Oksana wanted out. Oksana naturally took a step toward the door but stopped when she saw the guard was holding a tranquilizer gun pointed in her direction. Oksana immediately stopped herself in her tracks. The guard backed himself out of the room and closed the door.

CHAPTER 21

The Sikorsky Black Hawk tactical helicopter was flying low and on approach to a series of small islands. The helicopter stopped and hovered about 50 yards offshore of the further most island to the south.

Inside the helicopter, Kyle was checking his weapon. He checked the slide on his Beretta M9 and made sure there was a round in the port, put the safety on, then slipped his gun into his shoulder harness.

Casey's four-man assault team was locked and loaded and ready to execute. Casey's men were handpicked just for this assignment. Although this was their first assignment together as a unit, they had been training for weeks as a team and all had extensive specials ops training.

Casey leaned into Kyle. "With what little intel we have, the island just to the north of this one is our target, so we'll be getting out here."

Casey looked at the gear hanging off Kyle's backpack and thought he had gone way overboard on what was essential for the assignment. "Do you think you have enough gear?"

"I heard that NuFa stands for nuclear fallout. Thought I'd bring a little extra protection."

"You mean like, sunblock 3000? This place has been decommissioned for years. Funding for this site was cut long ago, about the time of 9-11."

Kyle and Aiko looked ahead at the nearest island and with all the jungle growth, they didn't see a place to land. From what Kyle could tell, the shoreline was only about 20 feet wide.

Kyle was curious, "Where do we land?"

"We don't," replied Casey.

As a helicopter started to lower closer to the water, the pilot, Cooper, flipped a switch that dropped a 15-foot Zodiac MilPro assault raft that instantly filled with air and hit the water ready to go.

The other two team members, Garcia and Hayes, who were already in their Rocket Diving Fins, opened the left-side door and jumped out of the helicopter. Casey reached over and slid open the right-side door then motioned to Kyle and Aiko to move closer to the open door.

"When you jump, I want you to cross your arms and hold them tight to your chest. Cross your ankles and when you hit the water, fan out your arms and legs like making a snow angel. This will keep you close to the surface and less of a chance of going deep and getting disoriented. The wash from the rotors will make the water a little choppy but my men will be there to help you into the raft."

Kyle reached out to Aiko who was still sitting centered in the middle of the helicopter's bench seat.

Aiko words were faint and insecure, "I cannot swim."

The rotors on the helicopter were in silent mode, but it was still noisy. Kyle and Casey leaned in to have Aiko repeat what she had just said.

Aiko took off her headgear and raised her voice, "I cannot swim."

Casey looked out of the helicopter and saw his men had already boarded the raft and had the Futura 40 hp motor mounted and already running. Casey returned to Aiko, "My men are ready to go."

Kyle put on his backpack and turned to Aiko, "I can hook you up with me and we can jump together."

There was no reply from Aiko, but Casey had a different plan.

Casey's plan was to wait until later, but one must always be ready to adapt. "I'm afraid that's not how this is going to work."

Kyle turned around and saw Casey was pointing his Beretta at him.

Kyle felt Aiko tap him three times on his back and Aiko used the shield on her headgear to reflect the sunlight into Casey's midsection. Then came a second set of taps but this time more deliberate. On one, she tilted the visor on the headgear slightly and caused the reflection to move up six inches. On the second tap, the reflection moved up to Casey's chest area. Then came the third tap, Aiko tilted the light up into Casey's eyes. Kyle used the distraction and was able to move across the small space and grab the top of the gun preventing the slide from moving.

Kyle threw all his weight into Casey and the two men scrapped with one another for dominance. Kyle's hand came off the slide of Casey's gun and in the exchange, Casey ended up firing off two rounds into the ceiling of the fuselage. The pilot of the helicopter felt the engine sputter and caught a glimpse of dark smoke drifting about, then another hard ping from the rotors and more smoke.

Kyle hit Casey with a right cross. Casey flopped back hitting his head, causing him to drop his gun. The men continued to fight. The helicopter pilot turned and looked back over his shoulder to see Kyle and Casey fighting. In doing so, he leaned on the cyclic stick enough to tilt the helicopter off-center momentarily, which caused both men to roll across the floor space putting Casey on top of Kyle. The pilot then needed two hands to fight the tension in the control and was able to finally level out the helicopter and bring it back into position over the Zodiac below.

Kyle saw that Aiko was still strapped in, "Aiko, jump!"

Aiko hesitated.

Casey freed a hand and hit Kyle with a right cross and Kyle responded with one of his own. Casey's head snapped back. The two combatants regripped and momentarily held off one another.

Kyle repeated his plea, "Jump!"

Aiko tried to release the seatbelt, but it was not unlatching. Aiko saw the gun but new she could not reach it without putting herself in jeopardy. The two used their elbows and knees as they fought for dominance. After a few blows were exchanged, Kyle looked over at Aiko and saw that she was gone. He swung his head around and looked past Casey and watched as Aiko leapt from the opposite side of the helicopter.

When Garcia saw Aiko enter the water not fifteen feet from the boat, he cracked on the throttle and whipped the steering around on the motor. He guided the Zodiac over to the area where Aiko was last seen entering the water. Garcia throttled back and coasted in a circle around the area where Aiko's bubbles were breaking the surface. Thirty seconds had gone by and Hayes was about to jump into the water to dive for Aiko when suddenly, she came up out of the water gasping for air. Hayes grabbed Aiko and pulled her up over the side of the raft while Garcia controlled the raft.

On the floor of the helicopter, Kyle and Casey's bodies were interlocked like a pretzel, both trying to gain an advantage, and both reaching for Casey's Beretta that had been sliding across the metal corrugated floor.

Casey elbowed Kyle across the face and was able to push himself off Kyle long enough to reach out with his free hand and go for the gun. Kyle grabbed the sleeve of Casey's camouflaged jacket and pulled as hard as he could. Casey felt Kyle lose his grasp. Casey stretched for the gun, grabbed it, and turned to shoot Kyle. All Casey could see at the last second was Kyle leaping out of the helicopter.

Casey squeezed off two rounds. As far as Casey could tell, he missed. Casey flipped himself around and slid across the floor to the other side of the helicopter, just in time to see Kyle take a deep hard dive into the water. Casey fired off three more rounds into the splash where Kyle entered the turbulent water.

Garcia moved the Zodiac in a large arc trying to see where Kyle might surface. Aiko looked up from the raft and watched as Casey leapt from the smoking helicopter and entered the water close to the same entry point as Kyle.

Once Casey was clear, the helicopter drifted north and tried to gain altitude but there was too much damage and Cooper did his best to make a landing on the south side of the island. He knew the beach was not wide enough but could probably make a shallow landing in the water.

Everyone on board the Zodiac watched as the olive drab Sikorski helicopter made its way closer to the island. With a loud bang, the engine blew, and one of the helicopter blades was thrown far toward the beach and cut a palm tree right in half before lodging itself into the side of an embankment.

Cooper had one choice, go in hard and go in now. Just as the skids took a hard landing in four feet of water, the rest of the helicopter's blades centrifugal force whipped the large helo over onto its side. The remaining blades sheared off and one of them went through the cockpit killing Cooper instantly, as another went through the gas tank causing a massive explosion, sending hot metal in every direction, and a ball of rolling flames up into the air.

Aiko had been holding her breath from the moment Kyle went under in anticipation of him resurfacing but when the helicopter exploded she couldn't hold her breath any longer.

A moment later, Casey surfaced. "What the hell was that!"

Garcia pointed toward the island.

"Cooper?" Casey asked.

Garcia and Hayes both shook their heads.

Hayes was hoping their loss was not in vain. "What about Morrell?"

"I didn't see him," replied Casey.

Hayes helped Casey into the raft and they continued to circle the area a couple of times, widening their grid search as they went.

Garcia slowed the engine to a troll, spotted some discoloration in the water, and pointed a few feet away from the raft. "There!"

Casey reached out and ran his fingers over the surface of the water and came up with a light tint of crimson that he swirled between his fingertips.

Aiko was disheartened by Casey's comment to his team, "I guess one of my rounds hit its mark." Casey motioned to Garcia to head up along the eastern side of the island.

About 20 yards to the west, a small hose was sticking up out of the water about 6 inches. Near it was a light crimson slick floating on the surface.

As the raft got out of range, Kyle allowed his body to float face up to the surface, trying not to give a silhouette. He was wearing a full-face mask with a respirator hose attached. He held the other end of the hose out of the water to breathe. With his other hand he was covering a graze along his left bicep he got when he took one of Casey's rounds. Kyle could hear his own breathing as he struggled with the flow of air through the small hose as he tried to take deep and calming breaths.

CHAPTER 22

The White House kitchen staff was hard at work prepping for the evening meal. Director Wintersteen had been asked by Chef Fassio to select the night's meal in advance as it was customary to try family favorites of the staff. Wintersteen, who loved seafood, was torn between an authentic Spanish paella or a grilled salmon. He had to go with his heart and he chose the salmon.

Wintersteen could hardly wait to get a taste. "Chef, you're going to have to show me how you get this plank salmon grilled just right every time."

"Thank you, Sir. Would you like a little taste with the pesto sauce?"

"You know I would."

Chef Fassio spread a small dab of pesto sauce on the plate with the back of the spoon then laid a small piece of grilled salmon over it. He handed the plate to Wintersteen who already had a fork ready. He got a small savory portion on the end of his fork.

Before he could sample the salmon, he heard agent Malone's voice. "I'm sorry, Sir, that's going to have to wait." Agent Malone approached Wintersteen. "It looks like we might have a lead on Majestic."

Wintersteen laid down the fork, handed the plate back to the chef, and headed out of the kitchen.

CHAPTER 23

Kyle stopped his swim as soon as his feet could hit the bottom and he walked the rest of the way onto shore. Kyle found a smooth part of the beach upwind of the crash site. Having landed in the water helped to contain the fire but left a hell of a mess. Kyle tossed his backpack onto a dry part of the fine, dense sand. He opened the backpack and emptied it out, tossing everything he now thought would truly be unnecessary, including the empty waterlogged Allegro cardboard box his respirator came in.

After quickly stripping down his military rucksack to the essentials, Kyle put on his green and tan checkered backpack and headed for the north side of the island along the eastern shoreline. He ran a few feet off the water's edge as much as possible for better footing. Soon he came to a jetty with a tall wide spreading banyan tree on it. Many of the tree's branches projected out from a central base. Off each branch was a series of limbs that grew downward back to the ground where they re-rooted themselves, forming more trunk-like features. Kyle set the pack down at the base of the tree and started to climb. It was like nature's jungle gym and Kyle got to feel what it was like to be a big kid. Once he got high enough he could see up the pristine coastline. After he looked in both directions along the edge of the mystical rainforest, Kyle realized he was about halfway across the small island. After working his way around a small lagoon, he would have about another 2 miles to go to reach the furthest most point, and beyond that, he saw another nearby island.

After climbing down the gangly tree, Kyle continued his quest to reach the north shore as fast as his legs would carry him. Kyle ran as close to the water's edge as he could without his boots getting any wetter than they had to be. The idea being, he would let the incoming waves flow in and the retreating tide wipe away his tracks as not to leave any signs of his existence.

CHAPTER 24

Inside NuFa 23, part of the nuclear fallout shelter had been partially converted to a processing plant. One part of the plant was designed to convert the processed cocaine into sheets of what looked to be the hardened chalk of drywall.

Kamiko and Jillian were standing in a small alcove that overlooked the processing area. A worker brought over a 55-gallon drum on a hand dolly and set it down at the end of a row of barrels. There were workers removing the dried coca leaves from another barrel, putting them into a pit where they were being mixed with a diluted sulfuric acid. Workers took turns in shifts stomping the mixture for a couple of hours at a time. The mixture was then heated to remove the coating on the leaves and filtered to remove the vegetable matter from the acid solution containing the cocaine sulfate. Once again, the workers stomped the leaves, repeating this process a couple of times.

Kamiko explained to Jillian, "The earlier shift of workers had already processed the previous batch by adding lime to the diluted acidic-cocaine solution. That made a soup like mixture that was stirred quickly and forcefully. Once the acid was neutralized, the coca solution was collected, mixed with kerosene, stirred, and then after being filtered, it was separated into a paste."

Jillian watched as female workers that were wearing men's boxers, a T-shirt, a paper mask, and a smock adding a thin yellow rope by weaving it back and forth at 2-foot intervals in a crisscrossing pattern. One of the workers then opened a cardboard box and removed a large plastic spool of cord. The box had a warning label and bold letters that read, Pentrite Detonation Cord. "Is that primer cord?"

"Yes, it is," replied Kamiko.

"Isn't it dangerous to work with such chemicals and explosives?"

"Yes, it is." Kamiko continued, "The coca paste is then purified by another pair of workers who continue the process, removing the sediments until the solution is colorless. The acidic solution is filtered once again that dilutes the paste and eventually becomes a dried chunk of cocaine hydrochloride. The previous days' batches coming out of the dehumidifiers is sent down a conveyor belt where tumblers crush the chunks into a fine powder. It is then cut with a bit of cornstarch and powdered milk to reduce the purity and add to the amount of weight to be sold."

Workers sifted the processed cocaine into a 4 x 8 preform, inch and a half thick, as it traveled down a conveyor belt. The last worker on the line added a specially designed handheld detonator to the end of the cord along with a matching receiver and a set of batteries to be installed later into the thumb triggering device.

The next stop on the line had the mold going through a set of rollers that allowed the cocaine to be fed into the mold and compacted down to the three-quarters of an inch. On the far end, the top form of the mold was lifted off the processed sheet of cocaine and sent on to the last part of the process. The paper backing was added to each side to give it the appearance of a sheet of drywall. As the densely compacted sheet of processed cocaine came off the line, a second 4 X 8 sheet was added to it, and tape was added to the sides to hold the two pieces together. Once completed, the double sheets of cocaine appeared to look like your standard sheets of commercial drywall bound for the job site.

Following the drywall as a completed product, it was sent to a drying station. The end of the process eight workers carefully added the double stack of finished product onto a wooden pallet to complete a stack of 20 sheets.

One of the workers then slapped a giant sticker on the side of the stack that read, MayCo Construction.

Jillian took a minute to wrap her head around the whole thing. "So, this whole site is a processing plant. Why did you bring me here to show me this?"

Kamiko replied, "This site is a gold mine, literally. Let me show you what business is all about."

Kamiko and Jillian took a seat in the back of a golf cart. Mr. Takata was the driver and led the ladies through a maze of hallways.

Jillian could not get over the size of the underground compound. "How much does a place like this cost?"

"It did not cost me anything. Your government paid for it. As a matter of fact, your husband gave me the keys. There is actually one more key I will need, and we are working on that," Kamiko said with resounding confidence.

Jillian still had no idea about the scope of the place and its function. "This is a government facility?"

"It was. It was built from scratch after World War II as a black site from the ground up, literally. The base of this island was brought in on barges and dumped in the shallow waters around a smaller island, expanding the square footage to meet the needs of the base."

"What kind of base?"

"A nuclear fallout shelter, complete facilities to sustain itself and one-hundred people for a year. They laid in everything they needed before bringing in more barges filled with dirt and buried the entire site. Then additional barges full of indigenous plant life were brought in and then it was left to mother nature to do the rest."

Mr. Takata stopped the golf cart at the end of the large cement corridor between the cocaine processing and a large vault. The vault had a very large door with a key code entry pad on either side.

The First Lady had heard of black sites before but thought she herself would never see one. "Why would my husband give you control of this operation?"

"He really didn't have a choice."

CHAPTER 25

At long last, Kyle had reached the north shore of the smaller of the two islands. He stopped his run by dropping to his knees to catch his breath. He removed his backpack and set it on the sand. Kyle noticed an oddly shaped shadow with a square edge on the ground next to his bag. He looked up to see the source of the 90° angle. High above, Kyle saw a camouflaged platform that could possibly be large enough to be used as a helicopter landing pad but didn't have time to investigate.

Kyle's mind was still reeling from his run where he was spinning scenarios through his head of what Aiko must be going through. Does she believe he is truly dead or did she have enough faith in her heart that she could sense he was still alive? Has she lost hope in him? The one thing Kyle knew to be true was he loved Aiko with all his heart. He knew when he was with her, he finally knew the man he wanted to be. It was killing him, the pain she might be going through thinking he was dead and he had left her and Oksana to possibly suffer a death that would never be accounted for. He remembered Aiko telling him that every life had meaning and there were two kinds of death, those who died with honor and those who died without. From that day forward, Kyle knew he would do anything he could to help Aiko to restore her family honor. For the love he finally found with her, he knew he owed her for teaching him forgiveness and moving on in order to find happiness, and that is what he focused on to find the strength to carry on.

Kyle looked across the water toward the island designated NuFa 23 to the north and it appeared to be about 200 yards away. While catching his breath, Kyle removed his boots and pants, then stuffed the items into his backpack.

Kyle opened a side pocket on the backpack and took out an energy bar and a small plastic bottle of water to consume while he gathered himself before attempting the long swim.

*****

The Zodiac carrying the assault team and Aiko arrived at the entrance of the hidden entry. Casey pressed a button on his walkie-talkie causing it to squawk. A moment later, the door rose enough to allow the Zodiac to enter. Casey hit the throttle and the skiff skimmed across the water into the hidden lair. The door closed behind it.

CHAPTER 26

Jillian watched as Kamiko was talking to a couple of the guards in front of the vault. She stepped from the golf cart and right on cue, Mr. Takata drove the electric cart away, and down another tunnel as everyone else gathered in front of the vault. Jillian looked up at the large vault door and security pads. Next to one of the keypads was a phone that was a hardwired satellite phone.

Jillian had recognized the locks from photos she had seen on her husband's desk. "A two-lock system, like those used in a missile silo."

"That is correct," Kamiko said. "It takes a set of keys and a set of corresponding numbers."

"Again, why am I here?"

"Why Jillian, you're going to help me open the vault."

"I don't have any access to such codes."

Kamiko pulled out a card, known as a biscuit, which had a set of seven numbers printed on it. She lightly waved the biscuit, "These numbers represent so much more than what this vault contains, something your husband has been willing to kill for."

Kamiko had Jillian's attention now.

Kamiko continued, "You see, every man has his priorities, and once you know what they are, you can manipulate him."

"My husband's priorities are to the United States of America and his family."

"That is very patriotic of you but the furthest from the truth. There are only three people left alive who know the contents of this vault. Myself, Mr. Takata here, and your husband."

"If you have both keys and the corresponding numbers, then why do you need me to help you open the vault?"

"Because you are going to call your husband and ask him which of these seven numbers is the right one."

"Why can't you just try them all?"

"Why Lady Dalton, I guess you know what I know. If I were to key in the wrong number, the locking mechanism would be disarmed."

"Who's to say he's going to give me the right code?"

"Because he knows there is more on the disc that I have in my possession than a copy of these key codes."

Mr. Takata returned with Oksana in the golf cart. Kamiko nodded to Mr. Takata who in turn opened a satchel and pulled out a Manila envelope. He reached the envelope out to Jillian who took it.

Jillian slid out a set of black and white photographs of then Sen. Dalton tied spread eagled to a bed and a naked woman straddling him. She had heard rumors that her husband may have been with another woman, but she was reassured by her husband it was all a smear campaign contrived by one of the other candidates running against him in the primaries. Now, looking at these photographs had she been wrong thinking her husband was a man of the people or had he actually been compromised this whole time?

Kamiko turned the knife. "What's the matter? Don't you recognize Oksana's mother?"

Oksana got out of the golf cart and joined Jillian to look at the pictures. There were a dozen pictures showing a beautiful dark-haired woman on top of her husband and from the looks of it, her husband with his eyes closed was in for the ride of his life.

Kamiko knew she hit a nerve. "You know we can't let these pictures see the light of day or your husband will no longer be able to pursue his priorities to the United States of America and his family."

Jillian and Oksana continued to study the photographs.

"Is that my mother?" Oksana asked.

Jillian slipped the pictures back into the envelope knowing she would never be able to look at her husband the same way again. Had this been the only one or were there others? It didn't matter because if these images were authentic, the last fifteen years of their marriage had been a lie.

Kamiko had all the cards, "If it makes you feel any better, he was sedated but as you know, pictures can tell a thousand words."

Oksana was feeling conflicted. She had left the thoughts of losing her mother behind and was living in the moment with Aiko and Kyle as her family. Seeing the pictures of her mother brought back the memories of the day her mother was killed in that dingy old hotel room. Those images of her with that man she now knows was Dalton before he had become the president, had found an emptiness inside her that was hidden by the life she had found with Aiko as the woman she now looked up to. It had taken her a long time to come to peace with never having the chance to see her mother again. Seeing her mother so young then made her heart feel heavy but it also helped to close that door.

Kamiko was becoming impatient with Jillian. "Now pick up the phone and talk to your husband."

Jillian put her hand on the phone but hesitated before lifting it off its cradle.

Kamiko knew she finally had everything in place. "Time to find out your husband's worth in the scheme of things."

Jillian's hand was still frozen to the phone.

Kamiko pressed on, "If he is willing to negotiate for you or just gives you the number, either way, you will have your answer."

Jillian picked up the phone. There was a flat dial tone followed by a double pulsating ringing on the other end.

Kamiko was in full control. "It's a direct line to the Oval Office. If you are thinking about trying to keep him on the line long enough for him to trace the call, not to worry, he already knows you are here."

The ringing on the phone echoed Jillian's heartbeat then there was a moment of silence on the other end of the phone.

Pres. Dalton's voice came over the phone. "You're not going to get away with this you bitch."

Jillian pointed the phone in Kamiko's direction. "It's for you."

Kamiko was done playing, "Let's find out what he cares about the most. His reputation or his family. Ask him, which code do we use?"

*****

Dalton was losing his patience waiting for a response. He was tired of having someone in the position to control him. Always waiting for that moment when they wouldn't even have to show their cards, they'd go all in, and even if you knew you had the better hand all you could do was fold. Then he heard someone very unexpected on the other end of the line.

Jillian was about to find out if what Kamiko had said was true. Was her husband the reason she was here? "Which number opens the vault?"

Dalton turned his head side to side trying to release the tension in his neck. His demeanor changed. His words were cold, "My designation is the third number from the top." Dalton walked over to his Toscano Old World Italian mini bar, poured himself a Jack Daniel's single barrel whiskey on the rocks from his home state of Tennessee, then dropped the burner phone into the clear pitcher of ice water.

*****

All eyes were on Jillian when those watching saw her anguish. Jillian's body language told it all when upon hearing her husband's voice, she exhaled, and her shoulders dropped along with her pride.

Jillian hung up the phone. "It's the fourth number from the top."

Jillian stepped away from the vault. When she turned, she saw Casey walking up with Aiko in tow.

Oksana dropped the envelope holding the incriminating photographs and ran over to Aiko and gave her a big hug. Jillian joined them and leaned into Aiko.

Aiko asked Jillian, "Where did they get the keys and the second set of numbers?"

"I don't know. They must have someone else on the inside."

Oksana asked, "Where's Kyle?"

Aiko didn't have an answer. She did not want to have to give in to the possibility that Kyle was dead and must be the one to explain to Oksana that there was nothing she could have done to save him. When, in reality, she was the one who left him behind when she leapt from the helicopter first.

It was the first time she went against her own instincts and did what was asked by the man she had given her heart to. The thought of losing him made her ache so deeply she knew this could only be described as never again seeing the one who showed you for the first-time what love was all about. Sacrifice.

Casey handed Aiko and Oksana off to his team members, Garcia and Hayes. Casey joined Kamiko who handed Casey one of the keys along with a second biscuit with a list of seven numbers on it.

Kamiko and Casey each took a position on either side of the large vault. The reinforced steel door was eight feet high and four feet across. It had a six handled wheel to release the two large outer pinions that bolted the door in place.

Having taken their positions in front of a key panel on either side of the door, Kamiko inserted her key, entered the fifth number down on her card. She could feel her heart starting to quicken as she entered the ICBM launch style command key into its portal. A yellow light on her panel lit up.

Casey entered his key.

Kamiko reminded Casey, "You must enter your numbers first before the key."

Kamiko held up four fingers to Casey. Casey removed the command key. He began to enter the eight digits of the fourth number down on the card.

By asking Jillian, Kamiko knew to play to her mistrust, "You realize this complex is a fallout shelter with full fail-safe measures. If the wrong number is entered, the vault will seal, and a 10-minute timer will start a self-destruct sequence that you do not want to be around for."

Casey entered the sixth number of the eight-digit code.

Jillian looked at Oksana's face and could see she had her father's eyes. Dalton's eyes.

Casey entered the seventh number.

Jillian had to put aside her hatred and give Oksana a chance to live a life without fear of living in her father's shadow.

Jillian yelled, "Stop!"

Casey's finger was right above the eighth button.

Kamiko grabbed Jillian firmly by the throat. Oksana moved towards Kamiko but was restrained to hold her position by Aiko. Losing her breath and her knees weakening, Jillian started to drop to the ground as Kamiko's grip was not letting up.

"Give me the designation code!" Kamiko demanded.

Jillian was still trying to catch her breath as she felt Kamiko's fingernails digging into her neck. Jillian was unable to speak but was able to hold up three fingers.

Kamiko released Jillian who sat deflated on the ground. Casey entered the third number down. The yellow light on his panel lit up. He entered his command key and with a nod he was ready.

Kamiko counted down, "Three, two, one."

Simultaneously, Kamiko and Casey turned their command keys. Both their activation lights turned green. The massive tumblers could be heard as they rolled back and released the vault door from its air-tight seal.

Kamiko motioned to Casey who took hold of the six handled wheel and spun it counterclockwise to a full stop. He then pulled on the large handle of the safe door and swung the door open wide. The stale air from inside the vault was musty and dry but it also smelled like something else, very old books.

The floor in front of the safe began to flicker as the lights from inside the vault come on and the fluorescent lighting failed to reach its full brightness compacity. A few of the light tubes were unable to come on which caused the remaining lights they were paired with to struggle to reach total illumination.

Kamiko moved into the light pattern on the floor, joined by Casey, then Aiko and Jillian were brought forward by Garcia and Hayes to see the contents of the vault.

A collective gasp came from the group.

Kamiko's words seemed to echo through the hush. "Now you know, Mrs. President, there are no more heroes in the world."

CHAPTER 27

Kyle stumbled out of the water and onto the southern shores of the island that was designated NuFa 23. Breathless, he worked his way onto the dry sand and found a large flat piece of rock to sit on while he caught his breath. Kyle unzipped the backpack and took a drink from his water bottle, then laid back on the flat stone to feel the warmth of the sun it harnessed. As the water cleared from his ears he could pick up on the solace of the jungle's percussion.

A light wind carried the rustling charm of the branches as they swayed in the trees. Kyle noticed the birds the area had gone quiet. Kyle was then startled by the rumble of the outboard motor of a Zodiac overtaking the sound of the waves that were crashing on the beach. Kyle quickly grabbed his gear and ran up the beach to a nearby cropping of boulders.

Kyle didn't have much time. He quickly filled his backpack with sand and wore it on his chest to use as a make-shift bullet-proof vest. He wedged himself behind a few of the large rocks as best he could. He peeked out and noticed he had left his water bottle sitting on the sand next to where he had been resting. He also noticed his drag marks in the sand from when he came ashore that led right to the water bottle. Kyle grabbed a nearby dead palm, pulled up his knees to his chest as best he could, and then rested the fallen branch against himself.

The two patrol guards that were in the Zodiac passed right on by as they continued their security sweep. For the moment, Kyle could breathe easier knowing they must have thought he was already dead. The men on patrol just happened to be on a routine search of the area and the guards did not take a closer look on their sweep to notice Kyle's almost fatal mistake.

When the sound of the raft's motor had faded, Kyle stepped out from the boulders and collected his water bottle. He looked up the beach in the direction from where the Zodiac came and saw the coast was clear. Kyle held up his hand to the sun to get a gage of just how much sun was left in the day. The sun's rays flickered between his fingers and the charms of the birds' harmonies returned.

CHAPTER 28

Inside the vault, a worker had just finished setting up a twin head Halogen work light on a stand just inside the door. He extended the bright yellow tripod as high as it would go then grabbed the end of the power cord and plugged in the work light. The large room went from a haunting dullness to vibrant, instantly. But nothing shined more brightly than the hundreds of bricks of solid gold. The gold bars were rough around the edges and had no markers of any kind. Their discoloration showed some impurities, but their value was unmistakable.

Casey rubbed his hand over one of the 27-pound bricks of gold and it felt like he was touching them all. That stack of gold turned out to be just one stack of four similar-looking stacks. Across from the row of gold bars was a row of cash perfectly stacked on wooden pallets. Four pallets, each consisting of one cubic yard of US $100 bills.

Casey slipped out one of the bills and smelled it. That was the old familiar smell he got a whiff of when he opened the vault door. Like a soft, light scent of vanilla, you sometimes get from an old book, except all these pages were the same, with pictures of Benjamin Franklin on them. The only thing that varied was the serial numbers.

On opposite sides of the walls of the vault were some of art's greatest missing masterpieces. Paintings from the Old Masters going back to the 1500s.

Oksana was in awe, "Where did all this come from?"

Casey had only heard about the contents of the vault but now that he saw it, he was ready to bask in its glory. "Courtesy of Saddam Hussein."

Casey began to walk through the vault. Casey continued, "In 2003, a coalition force led by the United States was sent in to depose Saddam. When our teams took the Palace, we found more gold and cash than anyone could have imagined."

Casey stood in between the stacks of gold on one side and the cash on the other, with his arms spread wide like Christ on the cross. "One of the teams in charge of removing the spoils of war got an order to take said deposit to a secure location for safekeeping.

Rumor had it that this was to be set aside to help fund whatever country that, at the time, could best help the interests of the U.S. on any given day." Casey gestured once again with his hands out to each side. "So here it sits, a 100% tax-free, off the books, ATM. A coup cash fund if you will."

Oksana asked what every adult in the room was thinking, "What's it worth?"

Casey took a quick look at the stacks of gold, "Let's see. Four by eight by eight, that's two-hundred and fifty-six bars per pallet, and four pallets. We're looking at over one-thousand bricks and in 2003, gold was valued at about $340 an ounce."

Kamiko had already calculated, rounding off a few of the numbers, "That's close to 135 million dollars."

Casey really got everyone's attention, "And in today's market, gold is three and a half times more. We're looking at just under half a billion dollars." Casey looked over at Oksana, "And that's just the gold."

Oksana's eyes grew large and even larger when she heard what Casey said about the money on hand.

"And it looks like a cubic yard of hundreds comes out to about 25 million so there's another 100 mill in cash."

Jillian was looking closely at one of the paintings. She hadn't recognized it but could tell from his other works it had to be. "This is a Van Gogh."

Jillian was right. It was a painting from 1888 called, "The Painter on His Way to Work". The other masterpieces were, "Portrait of a Young Man" by Raphael from 1514, "Nativity with St. Frances and St. Lawrence" by Caravaggio from 1609, and "The Concert" by Johannes Vermeer from 1664, all of which were on a register of paintings that were either lost or stolen, whereabouts unknown.

Jillian could see the dream but also the reality. "These all are priceless works of art and no doubt have been stolen, so you're willing to ruin your life over money and art you can't move?"

Casey had his argument, "My life was ruined in 2003 when my older brother's team was assigned to move all this here from halfway around the world." Casey collected his thoughts, "Right after that, they were deployed to take their next assignment, which just so happened to be a suicide mission into Africa." Casey walked up to Jillian and got in her face. Garcia and Hayes backed away. Casey's anger had venom, "How convenient. No witnesses."

Jillian froze when Casey quickly pulled out his sidearm and squeezed off two rounds each into Garcia and Hayes. Garcia died instantly. Hayes, all but dead, tried to raise his gun. Casey moved over him and fired a third round into the man's forehead.

Casey then turned back around to face Jillian who had just watched in horror as Casey executed two of his own men right in front of her. Without blinking, Casey faced up to Jillian once more. "Like I said, no witnesses."

Jillian had to believe that he really didn't think he was going to get away with this. She saw Oksana was clutched safely in Aiko's arms and said, "But you've got a building full of witnesses."

"Do I? As far as anyone else is concerned, this building doesn't exist. This money doesn't exist. When this is all over…" Casey didn't finish his sentence after taking a glance over in Oksana's direction. "Well, you get the point."

Jillian started to think to herself that maybe they could actually get away with this. "My husband knows."

Casey looked at his watch. "For only another 24 hours or so he does." Casey then walked away.

Jillian turned to Aiko. "Aiko, they're planning on assassinating the President."

"Yes, I heard. The question is, how? If they are planning to be here, who do they have there?"

CHAPTER 29

Kyle had made his way up the eastern shoreline of the island and stopped running when he heard the rumble of a Jeep. It was coming from behind him along the uneven dirt road that was semi-camouflaged, just inside the tree line. Kyle rushed up to a tree that was between him and the road and took cover inside some of the tree's exposed roots that had been exposed from beach erosion.

The Jeep passed. Kyle slipped out from his hiding place and made his way up onto the road quickly enough to see the Jeep turn a corner then disappear.

Kyle used the roots of the large tree to make his way up the hillside. When he reached the level ground of the road he began to run in the direction where he last saw the Jeep. He slowed up when he got closer to the turn and cautiously peered around it. There was no sign of the Jeep except for some dust swept up in its draft, floating in the shafts of sunlight where the Jeep had passed through the area.

Kyle started to search for the Jeep when he heard the muffled voices of two men talking. Kyle stepped back into the shadows as the two men walked out from under a camouflaged canopy and crossed over to a door that was hidden among the vegetation. One of the men casually punched in the door code as if no one was looking.

Kyle was about to step out from the shadows when he got a glimmer of a surveillance camera above the door tucked in amongst the ivy. He heard another Jeep could be heard approaching which caused Kyle to hesitate. Kyle quickly moved back into the shadows and got as close to the camouflaged canopy, as he could.

As the second Jeep approached, the driver hit the garage door button and the canopy rose up enough for the Jeep to drive in. After the driver locked up the vehicle, he walked out from under the canopy and hit the button on the remote once again. Before he could clear the door, Kyle clocked the driver from behind with a rock, and dragged the man's body in under the canopy just as the door finished closing.

CHAPTER 30

A colorful woman's scarf was draped over the top of a table lamp giving the room a nice moody and relaxing feeling to the space. The computer monitor was a contrast to the vibe with its harsher light emitting from it like a beacon from a lighthouse cutting through a thick fog. The screen showed an image sourced from the security camera where Kyle had just pulled the driver of the Jeep back under the canopy.

From the comfort of her swivel chair, Birgitta had seen everything the intruder had done but did nothing to sound the alarm. In the reflection of her monitor, she saw a vertical crack of light from her door being slowly opened and could see enough of the figure coming through to know it was Zen.

Birgitta casually hit a keystroke and the picture on her monitor changed to a darker toned screen saver of distant planets. The glass on the monitor reflected the office she was in also doubled as her sleeping quarters. She let Zen walk up behind her.

"What can I do for you, Zen?"

Zen moved in and looked over her shoulder. Not only was he able to see her reflection in the monitor, he was also able to get a good look to where her blouse was unbuttoned enough to show off a nice view of her cleavage.

"I just wanted to thank you for teaching me how to use the tranquilizer rifle and trusting in me enough to take the shot. I was wondering when we might be going out again?"

Birgitta teased back, "Going out?"

"You know, out to capture another tiger."

Birgitta enjoyed playing against Zen's lack of experience with a woman. She leaned back in her chair and threw back her shoulders, which caused the opening at the top of her shirt to close, hiding her cleavage.

"Can I ask you a question, Zen?" Birgitta leaned forward slightly giving Zen a slight peek at her cleavage once more.

Zen was being hypnotized, "Sure."

Birgitta switched the monitor back to a security camera shot showing Zen on the other island, south of NuFa 23. "How did you get over to the other island?" She paused, already knowing the answer. "You can tell me. Did you use the tunnel?"

Zen knew she must have seen him and he wanted to keep her trust. "Yes."

"You know the tunnel is off limits. It is not structurally sound, the security cameras don't work, and it could collapse at any time."

Zen's mind was on autopilot when he blurted, "The retrofit was completed last week."

Birgitta tried not to show her surprise as she slowly turned her chair around. "I've noticed you working out and relearning how to use the katana with less than a full grip."

"Kamiko says I can never be the master she once saw in me."

Birgitta stood up in front of Zen. She took Zen's hands in hers. She rubbed her thumb over the ends of Zen's shortened fingers where they had been sliced in half by Oksana's blade.

Birgitta worked her way right into Zen's fantasy. "I see the young man in you becoming that master one day. You can't let anyone take that dream away from you."

The two of them stood eye to eye.

Birgitta softened her tone, "I've also seen the way you look at me."

As much as Zen was enjoying Birgitta's touch he was really getting nervous and tried to slowly pull his hand away from Birgitta's.

Birgitta felt his hands becoming balmy from his nerves. "It's okay." Birgitta took Zen's left hand in her right and placed it over Zen's chest. She could feel his heart pounding like thunder rolling across the plains.

Zen had only dreamed about this moment and the reality was even better, but he wondered if Birgitta could feel the twitching in his hand as he cupped hers, "I…"

Before Zen could finish, Birgitta used her left hand to place Zen's right hand over her left breast. Zen released a sigh and she could feel the warmth of his breath pass across her face.

"Do you want to know what it's like to touch a woman or do you want to just continue to admire from afar?"

Birgitta let go of Zen's hands and placed her hands on the side of Zen's blushing face. She leaned in and kissed him gently on the lips.

"I've seen you watch the training that Kamiko's girls go through. Have you wondered for yourself what it must be like?"

Zen nodded.

"Would you like me to teach you how to please a woman?"

Zen nodded once more.

Birgitta slowly crossed the room and closed the door. As she made her way back toward Zen, she reached back with one hand and undid her bra. Zen was mystified that by the time she was back in front of him she was holding her bra in one hand and her blouse was still buttoned up to her cleavage.

This time when Birgitta placed Zen's hand over her blouse he could feel the tenderness of her soft breast cupped in the palm of his hand. For the first time, he was coming to understand what heaven on earth must be like. When Zen felt Birgitta's lips part his mouth and her tongue pass across his dry lips and made contact with the tip of his tongue, he was lost to her in every way.

When Zen finally opened his eyes and realized this was really happening, he awkwardly put his arm around her, and his hand came to rest on her lower back. Birgitta reached back and slowly slid his hand down across the high end of the cheek of her tight ass and back around to the front of her. She turned Zen and had him sit in her desk chair. She raised the armrest, so she could easily straddle him. Once she was on his lap facing him, she took his hands and helped him to undo the first of button on her blouse. With his hands slightly shaking he was able to continue on his own with the last few buttons.

When Birgitta's blouse hit the floor, Zen could feel the adrenaline in his body race through him as he looked at the perfection of her ample breasts. Birgitta cupped the back of Zen's head and guided his mouth closer to her small perky nipple. He kissed her and felt the warmth of her body on his mouth flow through him. She let him find his way with her. He kissed her from one side to the other and all around her neck. The smell of her warm skin fueled his imagination.

Zen had lost all sense of time. The next thing he knew, Birgitta was guiding him by the hand across the room, over to her bed. The space around her bed was dimly lit from the scarf covered lamp. As Zen sat on the bed, he got a hint of the aroma that was Birgitta, rising up from her bed sheets. The woman that was about to make Zen a man stood in front of him. He watched as she took her time taking off her soft worn-out jeans. One button after another was like watching a mystery unfolding and what was revealed was to be the gift of all gifts.

Birgitta stepped out of her shoes, slipped off her faded jeans, then took hold of the sides of her boy shorts styled panties, and guided them down over her smooth legs. Zen had only gotten a peek from afar of the girls as they showered but seeing Birgitta this close and tasting the beauty of her skin was amazing. Birgitta sat on the edge of the bed next to Zen and helped him remove his shoes, undo his belt, and take off his tan khakis. He was slightly embarrassed when Birgitta saw his excitement in is cotton boxers.

"Zen. Look at me. This is the most natural thing between a man and a woman so there is nothing to be that worried about. You're doing fine."

"But you are so beautiful…"

"So are you, Zen."

Zen knew she had figured out that he had never been with a woman before and he was just hoping that on this night, time was on his side. Birgitta took hold of his boxers and helped him to remove them. She could see he was more than ready for her. She positioned herself over him as she laid the full length her body over his, so he could feel every curve of her exquisite anatomy across his. She rubbed her breasts into his chest as she kissed him. He felt her legs part and her warm inner thighs straddle over him.

Zen found himself coming at ease within the moment of euphoria and the seduction of Birgitta's voice was more than soothing as it reached to his soul. "You are amazing."

Birgitta kissed Zen gently once more and he could feel her lips form a smile against his. Time had stopped and the only thing he could hear when Birgitta sat up was her breathing as it began to rise and fall, changing Zen's world forever.

CHAPTER 31

Dr. Leo Horst, a plastic surgeon, was in full scrubs as he exited the door of the medical lab. He pulled down his mask, removed his gloves, and tossed them away in the trash bin outside the door.

The six-seat golf cart carrying Kamiko and her guests pulled up next to the doctor. Kamiko had a history with the good doctor, whose scruples were of course, at the low end of the spectrum.

"Hello, Dr. Horst. How is our patient today?"

Dr. Horst was one of the few men Kamiko had come to trust over the last year. "She is fine. I believe the procedure took this time."

"That is good to hear, Leo. Thank you."

Kamiko walked on passed the doctor and gestured for Jillian, Oksana, and Aiko to follow her as she entered the lab. Kamiko passed through the stainless steel double doors and paused long enough to look the chart to skim over the day's procedures.

Jillian, Oksana, and Aiko entered the state of the art medical lab.

Oksana knew this wasn't your normal doctor's office. "Aiko, what kind of lab is this?"

Aiko did not have an answer.

Kamiko took the question, "It makes happy customers."

Kamiko continued through the lab as Aiko and Jillian continued to follow.

They came to a set of double doors marked, Recovery. As Kamiko entered, Aiko and Jillian caught the swaying doors and stopped in their tracks when they saw an enormous sedated tiger on top of a padded table.

Kamiko explained, "This is a Golden Tiger. They are very rare and can only be bred in captivity. When you have such a product, you can control the market, and that is what I do."

Oksana saw a curtain pulled closed at the next station over to her left. She heard a light moan but not from a tiger. She quickly moved over and pulled the curtain back.

There, in a medical bed, was a sedated young girl who had bandages on her face and breasts.

Oksana turned to Aiko who in turn looked at Kamiko. "You, are the animal."

"I, am a capitalist," replied Kamiko.

Jillian's heart was breaking. "What are you doing to these girls?"

Kamiko felt no remorse, "Giving them the best life they can have."

Aiko couldn't believe what she was hearing, "According to who?"

"My clients." Kamiko was confident. "When I get a specific request, I find the nearest girl to that request, and then with a nip here and a tuck there, I have a happy client."

"Why?" Aiko asked. "It can't be for money. You seem to have all the money you need."

"My clients want two things, power, and a woman to release that power on. Sometimes it just takes too long to get, and I help make it happen."

Aiko and Jillian looked at each other and could sense this wasn't going to be good.

"My clients pay top dollar to get that woman they just can't get enough of."

"And the power?" Aiko asked.

"They just have the illusion of power. I am the one with the power."

Again, Aiko and Jillian looked at one another.

Kamiko continued her delusional rant. "Not only do I give them their desire, I am able to turn that illusion in my favor. Powerful clients who got that power because of me. Not only are my girls trained to please their man, they still work for me, and when I give the order, they get a chance to be free of their confines by the process of elimination."

Oksana had a bad feeling, "Aiko, what does she mean?"

Aiko's heart sank, "She has trained the girls to be assassins."

Jillian was realizing the depth of Kamiko's twisted mind. "What?"

Aiko did her best to explain to Jillian, so Oksana could understand as well, "You have heard of sleeper cells, yes?"

Jillian nodded.

Aiko furthered her notion, "The moment her clients bought their fantasy, they also sealed their fates. They have their own assailant lying right next to them. All they are waiting for is the order to kill."

With all the attention on Kamiko, no one noticed when Casey had walked up behind them. That was until Kamiko gave Casey a nod. At that moment, Casey walked up to Aiko and pulled her away from Oksana.

Oksana cried out, "Where are you taking her?"

Oksana went after Casey and started to beat on him. Aiko pulled Oksana off Casey.

Aiko knew she needed Oksana to stay behind for her own safety. "Oksana, I need you to be strong and take care of the First Lady. Can you do that for me?"

Oksana went over to Kamiko. "You can't do this."

Kamiko already had a plan. "You're right. I'll let fate decide."

CHAPTER 32

There were two empty 55-gallon drums with the lids off sitting on the loading dock. About 10 inches down from the top of the rim there were 3-inch holes approximately a foot apart all around the barrel. The dock worker swung the pickaxe, striking another hole into the side of the barrel. The pointed end of the pickaxe head was jammed in the barrel and it took a good effort to jerk the axe out.

Casey was tired of waiting. "That's enough." The dock worker then leaned the pickaxe handle against the barrel. "Put her in," Casey ordered.

Two dock workers lifted Aiko into one of the barrels.

Oksana started to cry and turned to Kamiko. "You're her mother! You can't let him do this!"

Kamiko, without remorse, "Why the tears? Aiko is not your mother."

Oksana screamed out with pride, "She is to me!"

Aiko stood strong and was touched. "Oksana look at me."

Once Aiko had Oksana's attention she then looked at Kamiko. "You have to promise me you will let Jillian take Oksana off this island."

"I cannot make that promise. I have made deal with the President. The First Lady is not leaving this island."

Mr. Takata snickered.

Kamiko still had an axe to grind. "Trust is such a hard thing to come by these days. Take Mr. Takata here." After a moment, Kamiko made it an order, "Take Mr. Takata."

Two dock workers on either side of Mr. Takata grabbed him by each arm and led him over to the second barrel.

Mr. Takata was caught off guard. "What are you doing?"

The men each grabbed a leg and loaded Mr. Takata into the second barrel.

Takata was in a full-on panic. "Why are you doing this? I have been more than faithful to you, Kamiko-san!"

"Casey has informed me that it was you who gave away our location and led his team here to this island."

"I did no such thing! He is lying!"

"Is he? Was it not your responsibility to make sure no one could track our movements of the First Lady?"

Mr. Takata paused to go over in his mind the giving of explicit orders to the men he was paid to hire and set up the First Lady's abduction at the airport. Detail after detail went by and to his recollection, everything went off according to plan, right down to the implementation of the frequency jammer.

Kamiko continued, "Did you not let the First Lady and Oksana walk out of the isolated container on the ship, allowing their tracking signals to be picked up by satellite?"

There it was. The jammer was isolated within the container. "It wasn't my fault! I'm telling you, it wasn't my fault!"

Kamiko knew he had no response she was willing to accept. "Look around you. If not you, then who?"

Mr. Takata began to panic and freak out, "No! No! No!"

One of the dock workers had picked up the axe and pistol-whipped Takata with the wooden handle. The two workers pushed Takata's body down into the barrel, dropped on the lid, and strapped on the drum locking ring.

CHAPTER 33

Outside the entrance of NuFa 23, Kyle was now wearing the military camouflaged jacket and hat of the driver he had subdued. Kyle walked up to the entrance of the facility and kept his head down as not to show his face on the security camera. He took a moment to recall the pattern of the four-digit code the previous men had used to enter. He was pretty sure he had it and pressed in the door code. The door's lock clicked. Kyle entered.

Kyle moved along the interior hallway as if he belonged. He heard someone coming and pulled down the rim of his cap. He saw the woman walking his direction was wearing an ID badge on a lanyard around her neck. Kyle thought about it and remembered that the man he took the clothes from did have such a badge and he had left it sitting on the hood of the Jeep. All Kyle could do to not be confronted was to take the first door he came to. The recovery room was large enough to hold four hospital beds, full bathroom facilities, and a closet of supplies. All four beds seemed to be occupied with girls, all in their late teens/early 20s, all sedated, and all in different stages of either prep for or recovery from surgery.

Kyle cautiously checked behind the first curtain and saw a girl that looked to be about eighteen or nineteen with post-surgery bandages on her face. He checked the IV bag on the stand that was keeping her comfortable and heavily sedated. It was full. Either she just came out of surgery or someone had just recently changed it. On the nightstand next to her bed was some bottled water and a bottle of unmarked pills. On the end of her bed hung a progress chart. He pulled the paperwork and saw that she had indeed just come out of a surgery for a procedure known as an East Asian blepharoplasty. A type of cosmetic surgery where the skin that forms the eyelid is reshaped and altered to create an upper eyelid with a crease to look not more American but less Asian.

Kyle quietly slipped into the next recovery space and pulled the girl's chart. He noticed, like the other girl, she had a first name at the top of her chart. The girl, Maxine, was seventeen and just had a breast enhancement surgery. The bandages on her chest were also post-surgery and were slightly stained with the brown betadine solution used to clean the surgical area prior to operating. Kyle flipped the chart and saw before and after photos of the girl along with the requested cup size per the client. Kyle shook his head in disgust as he looked at the image of a beautiful young girl, who did not even need the surgery, other than to fill an order. He brushed the girls bangs back off her face and kissed her forehead. His way of letting her know if there was anything he could do for her, he would.

As Kyle entered the third cordoned off space, he was surprised to see the girl was awake. He could tell she was frightened and put his finger to his lips, motioning her to stay quiet. Her face had a series of blue pre-surgery lines along the side of her nose in preparation for a Rhinoplasty to make her nose thinner and to remove a mole just above her upper lip. Kyle rolled a small portable side table back out of the way. He undid one of the wrist restraints that were keeping her attached to the bed. He was about to ask the girl something when the girl put her finger to her lips and pointed to the last curtain.

That's when Kyle heard a man's voice coming from behind the next curtain. He cautiously looked behind the edge of the common wall curtain and saw a doctor skillfully drawing blue lines under the lower third of the patient's breast. Kyle stepped back and returned to the girl who was attempting to undo her other wrist restraint. Kyle knew if he had any chance to save these girls, now wasn't the time, and he would have to come back later.

He motioned to the girl to stop trying to escape and to lie back. Unsure what to do she complied with Kyle's request. Kyle took the girl's free hand and started to put her wrist back into the restraint. The girl pulled away.

Kyle leaned in to whisper to the frightened girl. "I'm going to have to come back for you." He stood up and nodded and mouthed the words, "I promise."

The girl gave him back her hand and he returned her to her restraints. Kyle took a step back and ran into the portable table. Both Kyle and the girl could hear the man's feet in the next space shuffle. Suddenly, the common curtain was pulled back with authority. The doctor saw the girl elbowing the portable cart as if trying to get someone's attention.

With a dry mouth, the girl said, "Shui."

The doctor walked around the length of the bed and over to the portable table. He picked up the bottle of water, removed the cap, and gave the girl a drink.

The girl smiled and thanked him, "Xie Xie."

The doctor looked around and everything appeared to be in order, so he decided to return to his other patient. Then he thought he heard someone at the door and promptly stepped out from behind the curtain into the common space and saw the door was closed. After a moment of undecidedness, he returned to his current patient.

Outside in the hall, Kyle was proceeding down the hall deeper into the complex. Soon he came to a door marked, Staff Only. He entered. Kyle saw a tranquilizer rifle on the table and went through the drawer below. Kyle found a dozen tranquilizer darts and pistol.

CHAPTER 34

Birgitta's bed sheets were in disarray and her panties could be found lying on the bottom corner of the bed. Birgitta was only wearing her button-down shirt as she stood in front of Zen. Zen was fully dressed and looked like he was still out of his mind from having his fantasy of being with Birgitta go far beyond his expectations.

"Now Zen, we shared more than a few little secrets and if you would like to continue this type of one-on-one personal training, you can't tell anyone. Agreed?"

Zen nodded and floated over to the door to go take a shower and finish the duties that Kamiko expected of him. Zen opened the door and looked back at Birgitta with a special glint in his eyes and a mischievous smile on his face like never before. He turned to exit but before he could take another step, Kyle bull rushed him back into the room.

Kyle's momentum pushed Zen across the small space and had him pinned against the far wall. Kyle reached into his pocket, grabbed a tranquilizer dart, and jabbed it firmly into Zen's thigh. Zen fought for a moment then his body gave in to the effect of the tranquilizer. He slid down to the floor, unconscious.

Birgitta rushed to the door. Kyle went for Birgitta, but she had made it to the door first and to Kyle's surprise, she closed it with herself still inside.

As Birgitta turned around, Kyle pinned her to the back of the door. "Why didn't you run?"

Birgitta was being calculated with her response. "I have my reasons.   When I realized what was happening here on the island to these girls, I had to do something."

"And just what in the hell is going on here that you'd risk your life for?"

Birgitta looked past Kyle toward her desk. "Let me go and I'll show you."

Kyle released Birgitta. She grabbed her robe that was hanging on the back of the door and slipped it on as she made her way over to the computer. She went through a few icons and eventually opened a file labeled, NIGHTFALL.

She clicked through a few files with status reports and images of the girls that had been personally selected for assignment by Kamiko. "Not only are they training the girls to be high-end escorts, Kamiko is training them to be assassins."

"How do you know all this?"

"My father trained me and Kamiko has asked me to train the girls in special weapons and tactics. It wasn't until recently that I found out that she has taken her business venture far beyond bridesmaids and escorts. Apparently, over the last few years, she has put a few of the girls in strategic places with powerful men of worldwide influence."

Birgitta certainly had Kyle's attention. "And you know this how?"

"I trained them."

Kyle spun Birgitta's chair around. "Who are you?"

"My name is Birgitta Bogdanoff and my father was an assassin for hire who ended up working for the Masato family."

"Karl Bogdanoff?"

"Yes." Birgitta was startled that this man knew her father. "Who are you?"

"My name is Kyle Morrell and I was there when your father was killed."

Birgitta stood up and was furious. She began to punch at Kyle feverishly. Kyle outweighing Birgitta by sixty pounds quickly got the upper hand and had her in a bear hug from behind.

Birgitta was gritting her teeth, "You killed my father."

Kyle understood her grief but knew she was wrong. "No, it wasn't me. It was a man by the name of Victor Pankov. In fact, your father saved my life."

Kyle felt Birgitta start to relax so he took a chance and let her go hoping she would not start screaming and give up his location.

"It's Birgitta, right?"

Birgitta saw something in Kyle that made her feel that he was not lying.

Kyle continued, "I don't know what you've been told but someone's been lying to you and taking advantage of your grief for their benefit. I am telling you the truth. In fact, I'm going to tell you something that could really get us both killed. I'm a cop."

Birgitta began to slowly come around. She thought that maybe if this man was telling the truth he could help her get off the island and out from under Kamiko's control. "A cop?"

"Actually, I am a Portland police detective on special assignment with the U.S. government to help recover the girls being held here."

"You work for the President of the United States?"

"Yes."

"I just found out about a plan to kill your boss, the President."

"When is this supposed to happen?"

Again, Birgitta chose her words carefully. "If I help you stop the assassination of your President, you will help me get off this island, and set me up as a U.S. citizen?"

"If you can convince me when and how this is supposed to happen I am sure I can help you. Tell me, when and where is this supposed to happen?"

"Very soon, at your White House."

"And how?"

"Kamiko is using the same technology of breeding the exotic animals on the girls to make sure they get pregnant. She will use that to get cooperation from the men who hold powerful positions in big business and who are prominent heads of government. If they don't follow suit, they are removed from office the old fashion way, by the enemy within, and it's made to look like an assassination attempt."

"We've got to find a way to get these girls out of here and shut this place down for good." Kyle looked at her computer. "Can you bring up the schematics of this place?"

"Sure."

Birgitta showed a detailed map of the island. Kyle pointed to the NuFa 23 building.

"Pull that up."

Birgitta clicked on the icon. There in the middle of the schematic was a round icon. A black circle with six alternating black and yellow wedges. The symbol for a nuclear device.

"Show me where they are keeping Aiko, Oksana, and the First Lady."

Birgitta pulled up the holding room. Only Oksana and the First Lady could be seen on the monitor.

"Where is Aiko?" Kyle asked.

Birgitta pulled up a screenshot of all the main security cameras in and around the complex. At first, they saw no sign of Aiko. Then Birgitta spotted Kamiko driving a golf cart down one of the halls. She pointed to the screen and they watched as Kamiko stopped in front of her office.

"That's odd. Kamiko was just with Mr. Takata and Aiko down near the docks and now there is no sign of either one of them."

"Can you pull up the cameras covering the docks?"

"Sure." Birgitta tapped a few keystrokes and brought up four different camera views on a split screen.

There was no sign of Aiko, so Kyle asked, "Can you play these cameras back all at once?"

"No, but I can isolate the main one and roll it back until we find them."

Birgitta clicked down to the feed with the widest angle then reversed the feed until they saw four men putting two 55-gallon barrels onto the back of a small flatbed truck that had wide grappler tires. She paused the reverse momentarily then continued. Then they saw Kamiko talking to Casey and paused it again.

Kyle pointed to Casey, "That man there."

"His name is John…"

"Casey," finished Kyle. "What can you tell me about him?"

"He and his team are mercenaries for hire. He's been on Kamiko's payroll for the last year or so. He's been here as long as I have getting this site up and running."

Kyle knew something was off with Casey the closer they got to the island. He was way too calm, and his evaluation of the op did not add up. When Casey commented about what little intel they had, followed by how this place had been decommissioned for years and how the funding for the site had been cut, it just didn't add up.

"Keep going," requested Kyle.

Birgitta continued until they both saw Aiko. She stopped the frame where Aiko was standing in one of the barrels.

Birgitta could sense the fear in Kyle's voice when he said, "Play."

They both watched as Casey and his men forced Aiko to get down into the barrel, added the lid, and attached the locking strap.

"Birgitta, where did they take her?"

Birgitta began running through all the images from the surveillance cameras. There was an image of two men in the front cab of the flatbed driving back along the shoreline toward the camera. "Can you zoom in on the men?"

Birgitta maneuvered a small joystick and spun the top of it to re-focus the image. Kyle had no doubt that the man driving the truck was Casey. As the truck got closer, Kyle could see the other two men, one was riding on the back of the empty flatbed.

Kyle saw something in the distance behind them and pointed at the screen. "Can you zoom in past the truck and show me what those are?"

Birgitta zoomed past and got a closer look at what had spiked Kyle's attention. They both could see there were two barrels just inside the surf, sitting in about a foot or two of water.

"Stop." Kyle pointed at the screen. "There. Where is that?"

"That is about 100 yards down the beach."

"How do I get onto that beach without being seen?"

Birgitta pulled up the schematic of the overall property and pointed to the side emergency exit that was closest to that part of the beach.

Zen had awakened but was still groggy from the tranquilizer. "What's going on?"

Birgitta opened a desk drawer, removed her key card, and handed it to Kyle. "You're going to need this. It is only good for the interior doors and access to the tunnel."

"Thank you, Birgitta." Kyle started to leave.

"Wait."

Kyle stopped.

"Kamiko has a boat docked on the North end of the other island."

Birgitta looked over at Zen then back to Kyle.

"It sounds like she's planning on leaving tonight with Casey. Something about laying low for a while. I just hope you can find your friends and get us to the launch before they get there."

CHAPTER 35

Just down the beach from NuFa 23, there were two 55-gallon barrels that had been set just inside the surf. One was a little bit further out than the other. As the waves crashed on to the beach, the barrels themselves took a direct hit, down low. As the water wrapped itself around the width of the barrel, the water rode up the side of the metal containers and fanned out to a mist. The wind carried the mist into the roughly shaped 3-inch holes near the top of each barrel.

Water vapor fell onto Takata's face. The cold water woke him up from his daze. He was scared and confused. His slender body jammed into the circular metal barrel so tight he could hardly move his head.

"Help! Help!" Takata cried out in a desperate plea. The echo was so haunting from inside the barrel it felt like he was mute, and the screaming was coming from inside his mind.

Takata looked around as best he could through the jagged holes. On one side he could see another barrel between him and the shore, about 10 feet away. Takata could feel his barrel had started to lift a little as the tide drew out. It was like a hand pulling on the barrel then losing its grip, allowing it to slide slightly across the bottom of the shoreline. The power of the tide would show no mercy.

Inside the other barrel, Aiko was calm. She could faintly hear Takata's pleas for help. She felt the first nudge of her barrel from the rising tide as the waves were sweeping out to regain its strength and return with a vengeance.

Takata's barrel began to float and as the waves retreated, they caused his barrel to be drawn out, away from shore to freely drift. As the barrel lifted, it started to slowly spin around and rock back and forth. A wave hit with enough force to cause Takata to bang his head against the inside of the barrel, where the torn metal edges of one of the holes dug into his scalp. The cut was not very deep, but it was enough to cause a gash and he could feel the warmth of his blood run down behind his ear and down his neck.

Takata watched as the sun appeared to dance slowly as it moved across the horizon, giving him a sense of vertigo as the barrel was a helpless vessel adrift. He then saw Aiko's barrel begin to draw away from the shore with each relentless wave.

Aiko listened to the rhythm of the waves crash against her barrel. She looked out and watched as the water splashed up alongside Takata's barrel. She could see a few of Takata's fingers sticking out from one of the holes and could hear more faint whimpers. Aiko could feel the bottom of her barrel skid out across the sand more and more as it was being drawn further from the beach. Aiko was thinking about whether or not Kamiko would keep her word and not harm Oksana when a good amount of water splashed inside her barrel and onto her face. She had to close her eyes for a bit as the salt water caused her vision to momentarily go blurry. When she opened them, it was like looking through a kaleidoscope of sand and palm trees. She could sense her mind was beginning to play tricks on her and her impending fate was testing her faith.

*****

Kyle was running down one of the long interior hallways when he came to the junction he was looking for. The underground complex maintained a core temperature of 65 degrees. The humidity levels varied slightly based on exterior doors left open, but roughly stayed around 60 percent, about what you would find in a wine cellar. With his heart pounding and his mind still on saving Aiko, he turned the corner and headed for the exit door at the end of the long hallway that led out to the beach. Kyle hit the crossbar expecting it to open but the door did not budge. The door was locked. Kyle held the key card Birgitta had given him up to the door lock pad. Nothing. He rubbed the keycard on his shirt thinking it might be dirty and not making good contact. He tried it again. Still nothing. So, he tried swiping it and after a couple of passes with no results, he remembered Birgitta had said it was only for the interior doors and the tunnel. Kyle turned and looked up and saw a security camera. The small red power indicator light was off.

*****

Kamiko was standing in the doorway as Birgitta was seated in her chair in front of the computer. On the computer screen was a spreadsheet.

Birgitta skimmed over the various columns. "It looks like everything is on schedule."

Kamiko not only noticed that one of the pillows from Birgitta's bed was on the floor but that her panties were hanging off the foot of the bed.

It had not escaped her that Zen had an eye for her, but it was confirmed when she saw his shoes just under the edge of the bed cover. Kamiko caught a glimpse of movement from behind a three-fold partition in the far corner of the room.

Kamiko showed no concern one way or the other. "I would like you to check in with Dr. Horst and see when our new girl will be out of recovery." Kamiko started to leave but paused, "Make sure my Sat phone is ready. I may need to activate it a little sooner than expected."

"Yes, of course. Is there anything else I can do before your departure?"

"No." Kamiko paused, "Birgitta, I wanted to thank you for everything that you have done for me. You have been a real asset."

Before Birgitta could reply Kamiko turned, walked away, and let the door close behind her. Zen stepped out from behind the partition as Birgitta reopened the security camera file. She saw Kyle kicking and banging on the crossbar of the door trying to get it to open.

Kyle was exhausted. He looked up and saw the red light on the camera then heard the door lock release. Kyle pushed on the crossbar and the door opened. The wind off the ocean hit him like a breath of fresh air. It filled him with such resolve that as he ran through the doorway he could feel his heart beating like never before. He knew every step he took would bring him closer to Aiko, but he also felt his feet sinking into the soft sand, stretching out time, and time was not on his side.

Zen didn't understand. "Why are you helping him, Birgitta?"

"Because he may be our only chance of getting off this island alive."

CHAPTER 36

The sun was low on the distant horizon. Both barrels were now afloat. The barrel containing Mr. Takata was further out from the beach and sat lower in the water than Aiko's. With each wave, more and more water splashed into the barrel. The water level inside the bottom of Mr. Takata's barrel was rising, causing it to ride lower in the water. That made it easier for the waves to add to the rising water level more quickly. It worked like a progressive hourglass in that as the sand passed through it, time sped up.

Takata began to tear away pieces of his shirt and started stuffing some of the holes in his barrel. As he got a few of them plugged, a wave would hit the barrel, pushing two of the cloth plugs back inside. Takata immediately grabbed the soaked pieces and tried as best he could to refit them back into the holes. As soon as he did, another wave hit and pushed the ill-fitting plugs back in. Takata held a soaked plug in place with one hand as he found the wad of loose cloth with the other, then pressed it up to another hole. Between those two holes, Takata looked through a smaller hole and saw that Aiko's barrel was now free floating as well. Takata pressed his face against the barrel close to the hole to get a better look. Water splashed through the hole and into his eye. He let go of the wads of cloth to wipe the salt water from his face and eyes. When his vision cleared, every hole he had plugged was open. The one thing he could not wipe away from his eyes was the panic they held.

Mr. Takata's barrel was now filled a third of the way with water which caused it to ride very low, below the halfway mark of the barrel. Takata sat back and studied the fluent colors of the majestic sunset through the 3-inch hole directly across from him. A calmness came over him as he was able to focus on a single cloud. He used the sensation he was feeling from the buoyancy of the barrel to imagine what it would be like to be that cloud floating freely across the sky.

Aiko could see just the top quarter of Takata's barrel. She watched as the waves started to overtake it with ease. Takata's barrel bobbed taking in more water with each wave. Aiko could see the sun setting on the distant horizon as it appeared to be floating on the surface of the water. Takata's barrel bobbed up and down, blocking her view of the sun. With each rise and fall of the metal silhouette, her mind went into a trance-like count. Once, twice, and then only waves.

Water splashed into Aiko's barrel, hitting her in the face. She wiped her eyes as best she could. The water level in her barrel was on the rise. She looked out to the sunset. She was calm. The sound of the waves hitting the outside of the barrel had a substantial rhythm now. In between each of nature's heart pounding waves she heard something. She looked through the holes, back toward the beach. Aiko heard the faint but familiar sound again.

She looked further down the beach and saw Kyle running in her direction.

Kyle was running as fast as he could down the white sand beach. He could only see one barrel that was about 30 yards out and sinking.

"Aiko!"

Kyle could hear a faint reply.

Aiko's voice sounded like a distant echo. "Kyle!"

Kyle ran up the coastline a bit further before he veered off into the foam of the shallow surf. He ran as hard as he could until the water was above his knees before he dove head first into the center of the aquamarine curl of the oncoming wave.

From inside her barrel, Aiko saw Kyle surface and come up swimming toward her. Waves continued to pound the outside of the barrel as more and more water splashed in. With the water rising inside her barrel Aiko could sense it was riding lower and the outside water began to not only splash inside but over the top as well.

The waves were getting too high for her to see Kyle. Water started to come in from every hole in the barrel. For a moment she had a small pocket of air at the top of the barrel. Aiko tilted her head back and took one last breath as the barrel filled with water and went under. Once she sensed she was submerged, Aiko opened her eyes and could see the light dancing on the surface of the water, was about five feet above her when she felt the barrel hit bottom.

Kyle looked up and saw that Aiko's barrel had gone completely under. He was close to the last location he saw the barrel. After a few more strokes, he was there. He took a deep breath and dove. A riptide had shifted the barrel from where it went under. The dark tone of the barrel was blending in with the patches of dark rock and sediment that had been stirred up from the ocean floor. Unable to locate the barrel, Kyle resurfaced, a bit disoriented and confused. He was sure this is where the barrel had gone down.

"Aiko!"

Kyle felt his body being pulled along, parallel to the shore and figured that is what happened to the barrel. He quickly swam along with the current, then dove.

Under the surface, the water was clear enough for Kyle to see he was in about twelve feet of water. As he scanned the area he saw the silhouette of the barrel just ahead of him. The closer he got he noticed a stream of air bubbles rising out of a few of the holes. Kyle reached the barrel and tried to move it, but he felt his lungs starting to burn. He needed air. He tried to push it back toward the shore, but he couldn't. He went up for air. At the surface, Kyle came up breathless. He took a couple of deep breaths and went back under.

After Kyle relocated the barrel he used the barrel as leverage to plant his feet on the ocean floor. He hugged the barrel and started to walk it back in the direction of the beach. Kyle could feel the sensation of Aiko hitting the inside of the barrel as she fought for every bit of her last breath.

Kyle felt his emotions pulling at him felt the kicking and hitting from inside the barrel stopped. He needed to scream. Kyle turned loose of the barrel and came up for air. He realized the barrel was in only about eight feet of water. On this stretch of the beach, the water was a bit calmer and the waves weren't breaking as hard. He dove. A moment later, the top of the barrel broke the surface like a submarine coming to periscope depth. The barrel was now moving toward the beach. Then the barrel went under.

Kyle surfaced, took in a few deep breathes of air, and dove.

Kyle hugged the barrel and with a surge of energy he used every bit of strength he had left in his legs to push the barrel closer to the shore, like a football player hitting a tackling sled in practice. Kyle was close enough to the shore he was now standing on the bottom with his head above water. He fought for air as he pressed on to get the barrel shallow enough. The barrel got heavier as it broke the surface of the water. Kyle was able to move it shallow enough the water started to drain from the 2-inch holes.

Kyle squatted and looked into one of the holes. He saw the water level had dropped to the level of the lowest hole. He could see Aiko. She was not moving. Kyle grabbed the barrel and with all the strength he had he bull rushed the barrel another five feet.

Once again, he looked inside the barrel. "Aiko!"

There was no response.

Kyle pulled on the release of the barrel's locking strap, tossed it aside, and pulled off the lid. Inside he saw a lifeless Aiko. Kyle lifted Aiko from the barrel and as he was walking her to the shore he was already trying to do CPR.

On the beach, Kyle laid Aiko flat on her back and continued CPR. He paused and checked her pulse. Nothing. He began more chest compressions.

"Come back to me, Aiko!" Kyle was so filled with emotion he could barely get the words out, "I'm not done loving you."

Kyle turned Aiko onto her side to help drain her lungs. With an open palm, he pounded her back a few times and laid her back down. Kyle cupped Aiko's mouth with his and on the third deep breath, Aiko's body flinched hard and she began to spit up water.

Kyle rolled Aiko onto her side once again as she finished coughing up water. Kyle's hands sensed the pain her body must be going through as she fought for air.

Kyle felt Aiko's body filling with life as her breaths became longer and smoother. He rolled her onto her back and brushed her dark, soaked hair away from her face.

Aiko knew it was Kyle even with her eyes still closed. "I thought you were dead."

Kyle used his hand to brush bits of debris from her hair and neck area. Aiko opened her eyes.

"I know the feeling," replied Kyle.

Aiko sat up and they welcomed each other's loving embrace.

Aiko's heart was filled deeper with every breath. "I have never loved anyone like I love you, Kyle Morrell."

"Now you know how I have felt for you for so long."

Aiko coughed and took a moment to catch her breath. Kyle could feel her body shivering. He had her face the sun as he rubbed his hands briskly over her arms and body to help get her circulation going.

Kyle helped Aiko to her feet. He stepped in behind her and wrapped his arms around her, allowing her face to soak in the sun's rays.

"Kyle, we have to go back to get Oksana and the First Lady."

"We will, as soon as you catch your breath."

Aiko turned to Kyle, "We don't have much time. Kamiko has someone on the inside and they are planning to kill the President."

"Well, we have someone on the inside here. Her name is Birgitta. She explained to me that it could be happening in the next twenty-four hours."

"Can you trust her?"

"She helped me find you and I'm grateful to her for that."

"Do you know who it is?"

Aiko took another deep breath, "No, but Jillian might."

Aiko started walking down the beach back toward the fallout shelter. Kyle went to her side. Together they started out in a slow walk that eventually grew into a quick trot and then into a full-on sprint.

CHAPTER 37

Kyle and Aiko approached the same door Kyle used to exit NuFa 23. Kyle took Aiko to the side of the door, out of the frame of the surveillance camera.

Aiko, I want you to stay here for a few minutes, so I can make sure the hall is clear. If no alarms go off, head up the ramp. When you get to the main hallway, go two doors down on your right. That's the room where they are holding the First Lady and Oksana."

"What if you get caught?"

"Then more than likely they will put me with them and you will know where to find me."

"How do I get in?"

Kyle held up the keycard that Birgitta had given him. "I'm going to block the latch with this keycard. It should open all the interior doors."

"If it only opens the interiors door, how do you expect to get through this door?"

"I just hope Birgitta is still at the monitor and the only one watching."

"How will you know?"

"Only one way to find out." Kyle stepped into view of the camera. There was a long pause, then came the electronic buzz of the door's lock releasing. Kyle opened the door, slipped inside, and wedged the laminated key card in the doorjamb at the lock.

*****

Birgitta was at her desk watching the monitor. She watched Kyle as he headed up the corridor.

Unexpectedly Birgitta heard Casey's voice. "I expected more from you, Birgitta."

Birgitta closed the screen and rolled her chair back right into the end of the silencer on Casey's Beretta.

"If my father was alive today, you would be dead by now for what you did to me."

"I only took what was offered."

Birgitta closed her eyes. She could still remember the feeling the full weight of his body on hers. The odor his sweat gave off and the aftertaste from his shirt he had shoved in her mouth to suppress her screams.

Casey continued, "Kamiko offered me a night with one of her girls. I chose you."

"I was not a choice."

Birgitta knew her fate was at hand and hoped what she gave Kyle was enough to make up for her past discretions. "Well, now you do have a bigger problem."

"What's that?"

"Kyle Morrell."

"You know, it doesn't have to end this way."

Birgitta felt a bit of relief. "Yes, it does."

The last thing Birgitta saw was her reflection in the monitor. She was without fear and felt free of any burden. The monitor imploded from the bullet that passed through her skull. Blood stains and bits of gray matter slowly ran down the monitor followed by Birgitta's body slumping forward. Her head came crashing down onto the computer's keyboard.

Zen was in shock. "Why did you do that? Why did you have to kill her?"

Casey turned his gun on Zen who was standing in front of the scarf covered lamp next to Birgitta's bed.

"Kid, anything I say right now won't make a bit of difference."

Casey tapped off two rounds into Zen's silhouette. The slugs hit center mass sending him back onto the bed, dead on arrival. The lights in the room went dark. Casey had left the room and what light that was left in the room from the corridor went dark as the door to Birgitta's room closed.

CHAPTER 38

A guard was standing in the doorway of the room that was two doors down from the hallway that led to the beach. His hand was on the door handle as he was about to step away and let it close. Instead, he leaned back into the room. "Looks like your country will have a new President very soon, and there is nothing you can do about it."

Suddenly, the guard's body was thrust forward, and he fell to his knees right in front of Jillian and Oksana. He was followed through the doorway by Kyle.

Before the guard could react, Kyle had his hands around the guard's head and with a quick hard twist, the guard's body went limp. Kyle let the man's dead body drop to the floor. Kyle didn't hesitate as he removed the guard's gun from his shoulder holster and took the extra clip from the guard's belt.

Kyle looked up and saw that Oksana had just watched him kill a man with his bare hands.

"Kyle!" Oksana rushed to Kyle and gave him a big hug.

Jillian was relieved. "We thought you were dead."

"You're the second person to tell me that today."

Aiko appeared at the door.

Oksana released Kyle and ran to Aiko with open arms. "Aiko!"

Aiko welcomed Oksana into her arms. After a moment, Aiko looked at Kyle and Jillian. "We need to find a way off this island."

Kyle still had the schematic on his mind. "I might know a way or at least a place we can lay low until help arrives."

Jillian asked, "Where?"

"NuFa 22. The island just South of here. There's a tunnel connecting the two islands. But first, we need to find a Sat phone and contact the President. There is going to be an attempt on his life."

Jillian was well aware. "We know. There is a phone with a direct line to the president next to the vault."

Kyle stood, then paced for a moment. He stopped next to Aiko.

"We need to make this happen, and fast. We don't know how much time we have before the guard change. Time to make a call." Kyle took a quick peek into the hall and saw that the coast was clear. With hand signals, Kyle motioned everyone out.

Jillian pointed. "The vault is just down this hall and to the left."

Kyle took the lead and Aiko brought up the rear.

*****

Across from the vault was the end of the cocaine processing line. Kyle had the group huddle down behind it. He saw the primer cord and detonators used in the fake drywall, along with a box of triggers.

Nearby, two workers had just loaded the last two sheets of cocaine drywall onto a flatbed dolly and were starting to roll it down toward the loading dock area.

Two guards were in front of the vault. Two more guards walked out of the vault pushing a second flatbed dolly with stacks of cash on it. One of the guards from outside the vault went with the two guards moving the cash, as the remaining guard stood on duty at the vault entrance. The three men in charge of the money rolled the dolly down a long hallway and out of sight. From his position, Kyle could see inside the vault and saw three pallets stacked with cash and one that was completely empty.

Kyle motioned with two fingers at Aiko and Oksana, then motioned to the ground for them to stay in place.

Kyle moved in closer to Jillian. "Time to make your call."

Kyle continued to use hand signals to tell Jillian to go one way while he circled around the other. Jillian was close to the vault and she let the guard see her. The guard turned his attention her way and Jillian realized the guard was Javier.

Jillian froze. For a moment she was outside herself as if she was listening to someone else tell her about the guilt and shame that was coursing through her body. Like an emotional roller-coaster came the fire of rage that caused her body to want to fight back once again, like that night of unspeakable emotional horror. It was gut-wrenching, and she wanted to vomit.

Jillian took a deep breath and knew she had to stay strong. She looked into Javier's eyes and let him know he wasn't going to get the best of her. Kyle came in behind Javier and pistol-whipped the smug bastard into submission.

Kyle drug Javier's body into the vault and out of sight. Jillian was leaning against the wall next to the phone as Kyle returned.

"Jillian are you okay?"

"I'll be fine. I just need a minute."

The First Lady took a few deep breaths and regained her composure. Jillian picked up the phone that was the direct line to the president. She listened as the ringtones paced themselves. She tilted the phone, so Kyle could lean in and hear as well. Then the ringing stopped.

Over the phone, Dalton's voice could be heard. "Is she dead?"

"Are you asking about me or Kamiko?" Jillian felt a sense of vindication.

Dalton did not answer.

Jillian continued, "We have it on good authority that there is going to be an attempt on your life."

"Whose authority?"

"Kamiko's. Now that she has opened the vault, it seems your partner in crime no longer needs a partner."

Kyle took the phone. "We need to know how to stop her."

CHAPTER 39

Inside the Oval Office, Pres. Dalton was sitting in his chair with his back to the resolute desk looking out the window.

"There is something you can do. You can stop her from getting access to the money."

"How do we do that?"

"Seal the vault. Lock her out for good."

Jillian had her ear near the phone listening along with Kyle.

Dalton continued, "There's a fail-safe mechanism in place. It is activated when you dial in the wrong passcode. You'll have 10 minutes to get clear. Once it gets down to two minutes you will no longer be able to stop the countdown."

Jillian took the phone from Kyle and hung it up. She grabbed Kyle by the arm and dropped down out of view pulling him down with her. A dock worker in a golf cart was headed in their direction took a hard left up the main corridor prior to noticing that the vault was at the moment, unguarded.

"What's he talking about?" Kyle asked.

"If you press the wrong code into either panel and turn the key it will close the vault and start a fail-safe countdown."

"So, it would only destroy the vault?" asked Kyle.

"According to Kamiko, the fail-safe will destroy this whole complex."

"That would be one hell of a smoke signal. Someone would have to see the explosion and investigate."

Jillian took a breath. "You're not seriously thinking about doing this?"

"It would make one hell of a distraction and we would have a better chance of escaping in all of the confusion. I don't see any other way of getting out of here without it."

Kyle slowly stood up and looked back toward the docks. As far as he could tell, everything was normal. He helped Jillian to her feet.

Suddenly, Casey slipped out from behind the vault's open door. Before the First Lady could react, Casey ambushed Kyle from behind and had his gun square in the middle of Kyle's back. Jillian started to reach for the key in the vault lock.

Casey pushed Kyle forward and retrained his gun on Jillian. "Step away from the control panel."

Jillian took a few steps back. Over Casey's shoulder, she saw Aiko holding a good amount of the yellow primer cord in her hands as she quietly moved in behind Casey. Jillian took a small step back toward the control panel to draw Casey's attention to her.

Casey flicked his wrist and motioned to the First Lady. "I guess you can't hear very well."

"I guess you can't either," replied the First Lady.

Before Casey could react, Aiko had the primer cord over his head and around his neck. She used all her weight to pull him back. Kyle spun, grabbed onto Casey's gun to keep it from firing, and helped Aiko take Casey down. Casey started to lose consciousness from the choke hold. He released his grip on the gun.

It wasn't long before Kyle felt Casey's body go limp as he passed out. Aiko still had enough force on Casey's neck to kill him.

Kyle tapped on Aiko's hand. "That's enough. We might need him to find the tunnel."

For the moment, Aiko kept the tension on. Kyle grabbed her wrist and could feel she wasn't going to release him from the death grip.

Oksana joined the group. "There are more men coming."

The sound of Oksana's voice brought Aiko out of her lethal focus. Kyle felt the tension in Aiko's arm relax.

Kyle pulled the cord from Casey's neck and checked his pulse. He was alive, barely.

Kyle pointed over the spool of primer cord and told Oksana, "Bring me that yellow cord."

Kyle turned to Aiko. "Are you alright?"

There was a deeper response than she let on as she told Kyle, "I will be."

Kyle took the primer cord from Oksana and tied Casey's hands behind his back, up around his neck, then back down to his hands. Casey was coming around and Kyle helped him along with an open-handed smack across the face.

Casey struggled a bit but then calmed down when Kyle attached one of the detonators to one end of the primer cord and then showed Casey he was holding an activation switch. "Time to go."

Kyle guided Casey over to where the First Lady was standing by to one of the vault's control panels.

Jillian reset the key in the control panel and put in a new set of eight random numbers. "Are you sure about this?" she asked Kyle.

Kyle quickly ran the options through his head. "It looks like it's a do or die situation. We let her get away with it, and if we do…we die."

Jillian turned the key back to the open position. The vault door began to close automatically. As the door began to close, Jillian could see that inside the vault Javier had made it to his feet. He was dazed and was trying to get his bearings. Once he did, he made eye contact with Jillian just as the door had about two feet before it closed, sealing him in. He stumbled forward but it was too late.

Jillian said adieu, "Enjoy your money." The vault door closed with a hiss as the airtight seal took effect.

A clock appeared in the red panel with 10 minutes on it. The clock began to count down. An alarm sounded through the entire complex as red lights alternately flashed along with strobe lights down every hallway.

*****

Kamiko was at her computer in her office looking at a live feed of the hidden boat shed on the north shore of NuFa 22. She watched as three of her guards finished loading the last of the cash from three large black garbage bags onto the boat. The men then stepped off the boat and walked away from the hidden dock, then headed back toward a stairwell that led down to the tunnel.

A red light on the wall above the inside of Kamiko's office door began to flash, followed by a digital clock that lit up 10:00 then started counting down. Kamiko switched her screen through various shots from the security cameras and stopped on one that showed the vault door was close.

Then another screen showed Kyle pushing Casey, tied up in primer cord, down the hallway with Aiko, Jillian, and Oksana in tow.

Kamiko went to her closet, grabbed a go bag, and tossed it on the end of her bed. She crossed the room and removed the katana and the tanto from a display stand, leaving the wakizashi behind. She slipped the tanto through the handle of her go bag as she picked it up and headed out the door.

CHAPTER 40

Kyle had a good grip on the high explosive cord near Casey's lower back, just above where it was tied around Casey's wrist. Kyle was able to maneuver Casey by twisting his wrist which would tighten and pull on Casey's throat and hands in order to control the direction he wanted him to move.

People were running down the hall going in the opposite direction toward the dock as they pushed through the underground compound. Everyone else was following protocol and were headed for the supply freighter to try to get out and clear of the complex before the implosion of the site.

Kyle pulled down hard on the primer cord, like pulling back on the set of reins, choking Casey causing him to stop.

"Where's Kamiko's office?"

Casey flicked his head to the right. Kyle steered Casey right and down another hallway. They came to the only door in that hallway and Casey stopped. Aiko tried the security key card they acquired from Birgitta and the door opened. Aiko entered Kamiko's office alone. She saw the security monitor and an image of the boat dock. Aiko moved the computer's mouse and clicked on the boat. The image changed to an overall image of both islands and showed the boat's location on the island south of them, on NuFa 22.

Next to the monitor was a binder marked, Operation Nightfall. She opened the binder and flipped through a few of the files. At a glance, she thought she recognized one of the girls. She continued to skim ahead and saw a picture of someone who looked familiar. She flipped back to the beginning of the file. There on page one was a profile and picture of an eighteen-year-old girl named Sienna. The page showed progress notes of her training and scheduled procedures. The next page had before and after photos of the girl post-surgery with larger breasts and a slimmer nose. As Aiko quickly skimmed through the images, she could see the girl's evolution into a beautiful young woman. The last few photos were of Sienna going through military training and becoming an officer. The next page showed her in action as a Secret Service agent.

That was where Aiko knew her from. She was one of the Secret Service agents on the President's detail on Air Force One. Aiko knew she could not spend any more time in Kamiko's office. She quickly looked around and saw the last remaining sword, the wakizashi, in the display stand.

Aiko walked out of Kamiko's room with the sword. "She is on her way to the speedboat on the north side of the other island. We cannot let her get to that boat."

219

Kyle looked up and saw the clock above Kamiko's office door counting down. The clock's red flashing indicator lights read 7 minutes 48 seconds and counting.

Kyle pulled on Casey's reins. "Take us to where they are holding the girls."

*****

One of the large rooms of the fallout shelter had been converted to a dorm for the girls that were being trained, as well as recovering from cosmetic surgery to conform to the client's request. The room contained eight beds. There were four frightened girls ranging from the ages of 16 to 19. They were huddled onto one of the beds using each other like security blankets.

There was a buzz at the door. When it opened they saw Aiko's silhouette and presumed it was Kamiko. Aiko then stepped forward into the light. "Come with us. Now!"

All four girls pointed to the connecting door on the far side of the bed. Aiko quickly moved across the room and opened it. The connecting door led to the medical lab and Aiko was the first through followed by everyone else.

The same four girls that Kyle had seen earlier that were being prepped or recovering from surgery, were still in their beds. They each had one hand strapped and locked to the bed.

Kyle grabbed a key ring off Casey's belt and found the right key to unlock the girls. Each of the girls from the dorm room paired up with one of the girls from the medical lab and went two by two with Kyle as they headed for the exit.

As the group gathered in the hall, the countdown on the clock now read 4 minutes 37 seconds and counting.

The girls tried to head for the loading dock as per protocol, but Aiko and Jillian held them back.

Aiko spoke to the girls in Mandarin. "Stop. You will never make it in time. You need to follow us." Aiko then turned to Kyle. "I told them they have to stay with us."

"You're right. We'd never get them to the freighter in time. We're going to have to go for the tunnel."

Kyle looked down the hall and saw a freight elevator. He started to take a step and realized he was at the junction where Birgitta had her office.

"Wait. I told Birgitta for helping me, I would help her and Zen to get off the island."

Kyle handed Casey off to Aiko who pressed him up against the wall. Before Casey could react, Aiko had slipped the sword's blade about eight inches out of its scabbard and had the blade's razor shape edge up against Casey's throat. Just the motion of Casey swallowing caused the blade to break the skin causing a trickle of blood to start running down along his Adam's apple.

Inside the room, Kyle saw Birgitta's head face down on the keyboard. Her blood splattered on the monitor. A trail of blood flowed out from under the keyboard and off the edge of the top of the desk onto the floor. Kyle knew it had to be Casey and the gun he was holding was the weapon that took her life. All he knew was that when the time came all he needed was one round left to repay Casey for what he did to Birgitta. Kyle got a glimpse of a silhouette of a body on the bed. He took a closer look and saw it was Zen. Kyle kept thinking to himself, all he needed was one round.

Kyle stepped back into the hallway. Aiko took the blade from Casey's throat which was replaced by the end of the gun up under Casey's jaw.

Kyle made Casey a promise. "You're not getting out of here alive."

In which Casey replied, "Looks like neither are you."

Kyle looked up at the clock counting down. "We'll see about that."

Kyle led the Casey down the hall by his restraints as the rest of the group followed.

At the freight elevator, Kyle threw his weight behind Casey as he pinned him face first against the elevator doors. Kyle reached over and hit the down button.

"Are you sure this goes to the tunnel?" Aiko asked.

"Yes. I saw it on the schematics on Birgitta's computer."

Casey couldn't resist. "She went out a martyr just like her father, or so I am told."

There was a ding and the doors to the elevator opened. Kyle turned Casey around, grabbed him by the front of his shirt with his left hand, and punched him as hard as he could with a straight right. He could feel all four of his knuckles go flush across Casey's face. Kyle could feel Casey's nose break and blood splash back onto his knuckles. Casey's head snapped back so hard he lost his footing and his momentum carried him back into the far wall of the elevator. Casey hit the wall with a set of weakened knees from the punch, which caused him collapsed to the floor.

Kyle reached in and pulled the emergency stop button. He then backed out and let the doors close leaving Casey alone inside the elevator.

Kyle had other plans. "We'll take the stairs."

Inside the elevator, Casey regained his senses and was awkwardly trying to stand up. With each attempt, he was choking himself from the primer cord that was looped around his neck. After a few attempts, he was able to make it to his feet. He looked across to the control panel. His eyesight was still a little off and the numbers were a bit blurry. He was still able to make out the emergency stop button and saw that it was pulled. Casey moved over to the panel, turned around, and with his hands still tied behind his back he felt for the emergency stop button. Casey pushed in the button and the elevator dinged. Casey was trying to work his hands free as he stood in front of the door waiting for it to open.

*****

Halfway down the three flights of stairs, Kyle heard the faint ding of the elevator door and pulled the detonator from his pocket. Casey stood at the doors as they were about to open. Kyle hit the detonator and the cement walls of the elevator shaft held in the explosion from the primer cord that confined Casey. The entire length of the primer cord that had Casey's hands in bondage and was also wrapped around his neck had gone off in less than a second.

Without missing a beat as they made their way down the stairs, Kyle got in the last word. "I never really liked that guy."

"How far is it to the other island?" Aiko asked.

"I'd say the tunnel has to be about 200 yards across."

CHAPTER 41

Oksana reached the entrance to the tunnel first as the rest of the group filtered out of the stairwell. To the right side of the entrance, there was a control panel with a key card pad, a couple of monitors with some instructions underneath them, and a clock that was ticking down from 2 minutes 45 seconds.

One of the monitors had a split screen and showed the tunnel was empty in both directions. The other showed the station at the other end of the tunnel. Oksana thought about the unknown distance and everyone making it across in time. Her immediate thought was, no.

Oksana tried not to panic but she heard herself otherwise as she called out, "Kyle!"

Oksana noticed that Kyle must have injured himself fighting with Casey as he had a slight limp as he hobbled down the last few steps before he worked his way through the group and joined Oksana.

"Kyle, look! It says not only can the clock not be stopped after two minutes but these doors cannot be opened as well."

The clock read 2 minutes 36 seconds.

Kyle pulled the security card from out of his pocket. Oksana knew she didn't have time to discuss the options, so she grabbed the card and swiped the security keypad. The door's locks began to tumble just like the vault and a green light went on the control panel for the door at this end. The light for the door at the other end of the tunnel was dark. Oksana tried to pull the heavy hydraulic door open on her own, but it was difficult. Kyle grabbed the handle and helped. As soon as Oksana had clearance, she took off running into the large tubular tunnel with its 6-foot flat roadway bottom with key card in hand.

Aiko was now the one trying not to panic. "Oksana!"

Aiko could hear Oksana's voice echo off the cement walls of the large tube structure, "The other door!"

The clock now read 2 minutes 30 seconds.

Jillian looked at Kyle and Aiko for an answer. "What if she doesn't make it?"

No one answered.

Kyle decided that based on their only chance for survival, Oksana was going to have to make it. He ordered, "Everyone into the tunnel! Go! I'll be right behind you!"

Aiko and Jillian lead the rest of the group through the tunnel as quickly as they could move. Aiko could see the girls were helping one another as best they could but knew the only real chance they had was for Oksana to make it to the other end in time.

Oksana had a firm grip on the key card and was running as fast as her feet could move. The only thing she could hear, and feel was her heart pounding. Then something came over her, her training from Aiko. She controlled her breathing to help quiet her mind and focused on her goal. The end of the tunnel.

The group was moving as fast as they could with four sets of frightened girls. One of the girls was still a bit groggy from the post-op medication. The muscle relaxer that was administered had weakened her and she could not keep up the same tempo as the girl who was helping her to walk. She caught an edge and twisted her ankle causing her to collapse to the cement floor. Aiko went to help the girl as Jillian led the rest of the group through the tunnel.

Oksana could see the other end of the tunnel up ahead in the distance. Her breathing was calm even though she could sense herself getting out of breath from the long sprint. Her legs were pumping as fast as she could move them. The key card was still firmly in her grasp.

Kyle was watching the monitor with the split screen and saw Oksana move from one screen to the next as she passed by the set of security cameras that were focused in opposite directions, which he could only assume was halfway.

The group was stringing out as some were moving ahead quickly and others were struggling to keep up. Jillian was encouraging the girls the best she could, not knowing if they understood her. She got a sense one of the girls knew English because when the girl looked back at her, she turned, and Jillian could only surmise she was translating to the other girls to hurry. It seemed to work as they all seemed to pick up the pace a little.

Oksana's feet appeared to be slowing down a bit. Oksana could feel the other side of the tunnel had a slight upswing to it and the rest of the sprint would have a bit of an uphill climb to it. She felt the guidance Aiko had given her was flowing through her and she could feel the burn in her legs start to tighten her stride. But she still felt strong, hit another gear, and pressed on. She saw the clock on the at the other end of the tunnel as she got closer, but it was hard to read where it was in the countdown.

Kyle was watching the clock counting down from the monitoring station from the NuFa 23 side of the tunnel. The clock read 2 minutes 7 seconds, 2 minutes 6 seconds, 2 minutes 5 seconds, 2 minutes 4 seconds, 2 minutes 3 seconds. The green light indicating the door from the NuFa 22 side of the tunnel went on. Kyle knew Oksana had made it. 3 seconds later the color code of red numbers on the clock were highlighted by an orange band that circled the frame of the clock. The red and orange lights alternated, the clock read 2 minutes and the fail-safe was locked out. There was nothing anyone could do to stop the countdown.

*****

The front of the group was only halfway through the tunnel when Kyle came up behind Aiko who was helping the injured girl. Kyle saw the girl's ankle was very swollen and that the girl could hardly put any weight on it. Kyle helped Aiko to set the girl down. Kyle reached for the edge of the girl's gown and the girl flinched.

"What's her name? Kyle asked Aiko.

Aiko asked the girl in Japanese her name and the girl told her, "Yuki."

Aiko translated, "It means, happiness and good fortune."

Kyle instructed Aiko to translate to Yuki that he needed a piece of the gown to help bandage her ankle, so she could walk. As Aiko translated Kyle proceeded to tear away a piece of hem from the hospital gown the girl was wearing and quickly wrapped her ankle for support. Kyle looked up and saw the security cameras pointing in each direction that he saw Oksana run past earlier.

Kyle looked at Aiko. "We're only halfway and we don't have much time. We need to go, now!"

Kyle picked up the fallen girl, took her in his arms, and started running with her down the tunnel in the direction of NuFa 22.

At the other end of the tunnel, Oksana was between the open door and the monitoring station. She could see Jillian was leading the group of girls her way. She looked at the clock. With red warning lights flashing the clock read 30 seconds.

The group led by Jillian reached the door and Oksana helped Jillian get the girls through the door to the room at the bottom of the stairwell for safety.

Oksana was a bit confused. "Where is Kyle and Aiko?"

Jillian and Oksana looked back through the tunnel and with not much time to spare, saw Aiko, followed by Kyle, who was carrying the injured girl.

Oksana began to go back into the tunnel. "Kyle!"

Suddenly, the tunnel was rocked by an explosion. The fail-safe mechanism had gone off. The explosion and ensuing shockwave it had created was the same effect as a localized 6.0 earthquake. Kyle and Aiko were immediately knocked to the ground. The reverberations from the explosion finally settled.

Jillian turned to the group of frightened girls and pointed to the stairwell. "Everyone, up to the surface."

The group of seven girls was at first too scared to move as some small debris was still falling down the stairwell from the explosion.

As the dust settled Jillian pointed up the stairs. "Go!"

The girls paired up once more and started up the stairs.

The security cameras that were halfway through the tunnel had been knocked loose from their brackets and were hanging in place by their video security camera cords. A deep crack in the wall behind the set cameras had started seeping water into the tunnel. The seep quickly became a steady stream as a chunk of cement fell away from the cracked wall, making matter worse.

Kyle and Aiko sensed the danger. They could feel the tunnel starting to shift and water starting to appear through more and more cracks everywhere. Water began to spout as if a fire suppression system had gone off.

"Run!" Kyle yelled as he helped Aiko and the girl to get to their feet. Kyle grabbed the girl in his arms once more and they started running for the open door that was still 40 yards away.

The edges that made up the tunnel's seal at the far end closest to NuFa 23 started grumbling and in a matter of seconds, that end of the cement tunnel collapsed. Water rushed into the tunnel as well as the stairwell.

There was so much energy displaced it sent a burst of air through the tunnel as powerful as a jet engine.

Kyle and Aiko could hear the rush of water coming their way, and the air pressure in the tunnel building as they headed for the far exit.

On the monitor, at an obscure angle from the dangling security camera that was at the halfway mark, Oksana could see water coming through the tunnel like a runaway locomotive.

Just as Kyle, who was carrying the injured girl, and Aiko were about to reach the door, they were forced off their feet and blown from the tunnel like a circus clown being blown from a cannon, from the immense air pressure and the water surging behind them.

Jillian and Oksana closed the heavy hydraulic door and Oksana swiped the security card across the keypad and the door's heavy locks sealed the door shut. From inside the small room at the base of the stairs, which was a mirror image of the room at the other end of the tunnel, the monitor showed a view from the inside panel facing back down the tunnel. With the door closed, Kyle and Aiko made it to their feet in time to watch with Jillian and Oksana. The rush of seawater compressed the remaining air in the tunnel causing the walls of the tunnel to give way. They exploded outward with a reverberating crash that sounded like roaring thunder. The room shook, and the monitors went out, but the tunnel door held.

Kyle looked around the large crypt-like space. "Where are the girls?"

CHAPTER 42

The top of the stairwell emptied onto a hidden landing among a group of boulders that made up one wall of a large room near the water's north shore of NuFa 22. The rocks and landscape around the room helped to hide the building's true size and shape from any satellites looking down from above.

Not too far from the door, the group of girls were huddled together in a down pool of light coming from a floodlight that was mounted on the top corner of the camouflaged building. There was a full moon that added a bit of diffused light to the sky but the illumination coming from the floodlight cut through the darkness with a purpose. This was the same building that Kyle had seen earlier from the beach below.

Kyle, Aiko, Oksana, and Jillian appeared from the stairwell. Kyle recognized the area from a different angle as not far from where he went into the water to swim across to the other island.

Oksana and Jillian walked Yuki, the injured girl that Kyle helped through the tunnel, over to the group of girls to reunite her with the others, and to check on them. Kyle carefully worked his way along the rocks to reach the edge of the building near the water and looked around into the building. The hidden shelter turned out to be a camouflaged boat slip and inside he saw a 24-foot Baja go-fast boat. The boat's protective canvas cover had been removed and was lying on the deck against the wall, along with a few extra gas cans of fuel. Next to the fuel were a couple of wooden crates. One of them held life jackets and the other empty plastic fuel could be refilled. Other than that, the boat looked to be all prepped and ready to go.

Kyle got a bad feeling. Prepped and ready to go for who? Then it hit him, Kamiko. In all of the excitement, he had lost all track of her, and he had to wonder if she had made it out, or did she get caught up in the explosion? Kyle quickly turned around and started to make his way back to join Aiko and the others. Once he arrived, he looked past Aiko. Over her shoulder, he saw the group of girls, one of which was making her way from the back to get closer to Oksana. Except it was not one of the girls, it was Kamiko. She had used the darkness to blend in with the girls until she was ready to strike, and now she was. She stepped forward with the katana drawn and was on Oksana quickly.

The shadows from the down pool had disguised Kamiko among the group of girls but the blade had caught enough light that Kyle could see the danger unfolding.

Aiko saw the change in Kyle's face and turned to see Kamiko holding the sword's 30-inch blade to Oksana's throat. Jillian backed away and joined Kyle and Aiko. The group of girls started to back away from

235

Kamiko, but then she yelled out a command in Japanese, and all the girls froze in fear. Oksana saw the fear in Kyle and Aiko and knew by Kamiko's voice, this time it wasn't just a threat to control, but one of payback.

Kamiko made her pledge, "Your escape was only temporary. Your victory was fleeting. For what? Did you think by destroying this island you'd have stopped my business? There will always be a demand for what I do."

Kyle drew the automatic and pointed it at Kamiko's head. "I'm only going to say this once. Let Oksana go."

Kamiko showed no emotion what so ever. "Mr. Morrell, your request is based on a flawed theory. You think I care."

With cat-like reflexes, Kamiko took the razor-sharp blade away from Oksana's throat. She quickly reversed the sword's blade and forcibly straightened out her right arm with precision. The end of the blade sliced clean threw Yuki's neck. The girl's severed head and body fell simultaneously and only separated when they hit the ground. Before Kyle could react, Kamiko had the sword's blade back up against Oksana's throat. Out of the corner of her eye, Oksana could see where the light no longer reflected off the sword's blade due to the crimson discoloration that slowly slid down the edge of the katana's blade.

Aiko was filled with so many mixed emotions but could not give in to Kamiko's ploy to draw out a reaction. "Let her go. This is between you and I."

"Yes, it always has been, my kagemusha."

Kyle took the bait and turned to Aiko. "What does she mean by kagemusha?"

Aiko replied, "It means, shadow warrior."

The one thing Kamiko had over Aiko was her past. Kamiko knew it was the one thing she would never tell Kyle about. Now that Kyle had asked, Kamiko was going to enjoy telling him the one thing that could drive a wedge between his and Aiko's happiness.

"I trained Aiko myself to become the warrior she is today." Kamiko had her left hand gripping Oksana's hair controlling her head movement like a puppet. Kamiko continued, "Unlike the training, she taught this little one, I taught her not only how to survive but how to kill without emotion and on command."

Kyle could see Aiko was holding back and he knew why. He knew that Kamiko was trying to break her and Kyle accepted her silence.

Kamiko continued the verbal assault, "Kyle, you are familiar with the term, a sleeper, yes?"

Kamiko took Kyle's silence as a yes and finished her thought. "It is a term that means, a political decoy. It is a person who is taught to become someone else in order to have an influence on another."

Kyle was now connecting the dots between a sleeper and a shadow warrior for what Kamiko had been using the girls for. But what did that have to do with Aiko?

Kamiko saw the wheels turning in Kyle's mind as he changed his focus from Aiko back to Kamiko as she continued.

"When Aiko was born I knew the only way to give her a better life than I had was to give her up. In doing so, her father and I had to deny her our love, but we were not going to deny her fate. We gave her the best of everything."

Kyle couldn't hold back, "You put her in an orphanage!"

"With the best training in the land!" Kamiko retaliated.

Kyle wasn't arguing, he was trying to get into Kamiko's head.

"You trained her to be a geisha then turned her over to her father!"

"I trained her to be an assassin!"

Silence filled the void that led to the sound of the ocean quietly crashing onto the beach in the distance.

Kamiko could feel Oksana's head turn to look at Aiko trying to get some sort of reaction out of her, to know if it was true or not.

Kamiko continued her rant, "Yes, a killer. A shadow warrior. I trained her to be wanted by the very men she was assigned to kill if I commanded it." More silence as Kamiko saw Kyle thinking back to how and when he met Aiko. "I sent her to Portland to take care of business that her father was tasked to complete. Instead, he could not stay away from her like he could not stay away from me when I was her age."

Kyle had been standing tall but Kamiko could tell by his body language her haunting little tale was getting to him. One sign was that Kyle was no longer holding the gun at her but instead, had it down at his side.

"Like the girls, we were training here, Aiko's assignment was to stay in the shadows and to be there in case her father, Ichiro, could not finish off the police captain he had been blackmailing."

Kamiko felt the emotional energy slowly start to drain from Kyle's body.

"But then you and your brother came on the scene and tried to play hero. Then I heard that one of you had shot Aiko and that it was Hitoshi's blade that took care of Captain Morrell."

Aiko found her voice and it came from her heart, "I am no longer the shadow warrior you created and no

239

longer your daughter. I am the warrior who is willing to die for her loved ones, and you are not one of them. This needs to end. Now."

"So now I see where your heart truly lies."

"This isn't going to end until we are both dead."

"Only one of us has to die. After that it won't matter to the other now will it?"

Kamiko slowly drew the sword away from Oksana's throat and allowed her to slip away. Kamiko watched as Aiko drew her wakizashi from its scabbard in her belt.

"I see you are no longer afraid to stand up to your mother."

"You have dishonored our family to the point we are no longer family."

"What do you know about honor?"

"I know what it is not."

"So, what does that leave you?"

Aiko looked to each side and saw Oksana and Kyle.

"I have more now than I thought I ever would. My own family to honor."

Kamiko stepped forward and Aiko countered as the two women started to take a stance. "I guess they will have to learn what loss is as well." Kamiko leaned in with a quick thrust and the two warriors exchanged counter strikes as the blades of their swords clashed with full contact and power.

The group of girls backed away. Jillian and Oksana, as well as Kyle, stayed off to the side, but not too far away.

Kamiko and Aiko stepped in once more with an even quicker exchange of strikes, both showing grace and balance. As the two broke, Aiko's blade passed close enough to Kamiko's head to cut off some of her hair. To Kamiko, the missing hair was a sign of loss of balance and it momentarily caught her off guard. Kamiko quickly found her center, raised her katana with both hands above her head, expecting to thrust her anger down on Aiko.

Before Kamiko could bring the sword down, with her back to Kamiko, Aiko stepped into Kamiko's body. As Kamiko's arms came down, Aiko allowed Kamiko to wrap her arms around her. As Kamiko brought the katana up with both hands toward her face, Aiko used the wakizashi with both hands to block the blade.

Kamiko was impressed. "I see you have learned something on your own, but I would not have taught you to give up such a place of position and power."

"Victory is reserved for those who are willing to pay its price."

Aiko let go with her right hand and drew the tanto from Kamiko's waistband and slipped it under her left armpit. With only one hand on the wakizashi, Kamiko was able to overpower Aiko's block and pushed Aiko away. In doing so, her blade caught the right side of Aiko's ribcage.

Aiko stumbled forward into Kyle's arms. She placed her hand to her side and felt some blood soaking through her shirt. A lot of blood.

Kyle was at a loss. "Aiko, why would you allow yourself to get that close to her?" Aiko dropped the tanto to the ground that was laced with Kamiko's blood.

Aiko looked into Kyle's cyes. "One of us had to die."

Kamiko looked around at Oksana and Kyle, then back at Aiko. She dropped the katana and began to flex her hand. Kamiko had lost the power to grip her katana, "My hand…"

Kamiko had not felt the tanto's blade make contact as she pushed Aiko's body away from her. She was more focused on where her blade was going to strike Aiko. Kamiko raised her arm up, away from her body enough to see that the tanto Aiko had placed under her arm had also been under her own. Kamiko came to the stark realization that as she had pushed Aiko away, the end of the tanto's blade had sliced her inner arm, just below her armpit. Aiko's cut was deep enough to her mother's arm that it sliced completely through the brachial artery. Kamiko could feel her body immediately growing cold and her mind getting foggy, as her blood pressure quickly dropped, because of the massive blood loss.

Aiko knew her blade had reached its intended target, "You don't have much time."

"I know that now."

Kamiko began to walk toward Aiko. As she did, everyone stepped back keeping their distance. Kamiko's strength was draining with every drop of her blood. She took a few more steps then dropped to her knees.

Kamiko's fading memory was causing the events of the past, that should have been happy ones, were only haunting her. "I remember when you were a child. Your sensei and I agreed you had such potential and we were so proud of you."

"What happened to honoring the family name?"

Kamiko looked down and saw that she was now kneeling right in front of the tanto stained with her blood. Kamiko picked up tanto. "A family without honor is just a name. Now I must honor mine and go to join my brother." Kamiko raised the point of the tanto to her belly to commit seppuku, the art of ritual suicide also known as hara-kiri. Kyle was not going to allow Kamiko to justify her life and die in such an honorable way.

Kyle raised his gun and shot Kamiko between the eyes. "I don't think so."

Weakened, Aiko fell deeper into Kyle's arms. Kyle placed his hand firmly on Aiko's wound and held her side as tightly as possible.

Jillian had deeper concerns. "We need a doctor."

Aiko's memories were from a new place in her life. "When I was in the barrel, all I could think about was starting a family with you."

Kyle prayed his promise to Aiko. "And we will."

Aiko began to pass out.

"Stay with me Aiko!"

Oksana knelt next to Kyle. "Is she going to die?"

Kyle did not have an answer for her.

Kyle knew the answer to Oksana's question wasn't to be found on the island. "Everyone, to the boat!"

Oksana felt a sense of hope, "What boat?"

CHAPTER 43

Inside the boat shed, a couple of interior floodlights had taken full effect. Kyle was in the 24-foot power boat, helping the seven girls to board. Jillian was sitting with Aiko at the back of the boat having wrapped her in a small blanket helping her to stay warm and dry. They had wrapped Yuki's body in half the boat's canvas cover and bound it with some rope from the anchor. Kyle stepped off the boat and he helped Oksana bring Yuki's body on board. Kyle secured Yuki's body on one side of the boat's guard rail to match the same location on the opposite side of the boat, where he had secured Kamiko's body. It too had been wrapped in half of the boat's canvas cover and bound in rope.

Kyle needed to act to stay focused. "Oksana, take the girls down into the hold and help them to get settled."

They entered the hold and Oksana followed.

Kyle went to Jillian. "How is she?"

"She's lost a lot of blood, but I think the bleeding has stopped. But I don't know if she can take such a bumpy ride without starting to bleed again."

Kyle looked in the storage space below the passenger seat and pulled out a roll of duct tape. He tore off a few pieces and taped down the cloth they had covering Aiko's wound. He then taped all the way around Aiko's body to keep the makeshift bandage in place.

As Kyle finished taping Aiko's wound, Aiko came to. "Kyle." Kyle stopped and gave Aiko his full attention. "We can't leave her here."

"We're not leaving anyone, Aiko," Kyle replied.

Without knowing if Aiko had heard Kyle's reply, Aiko faded into unconsciousness.

Oksana returned from the hold. "Kyle."

Kyle turned around and saw Oksana holding Kamiko's satchel in one hand and a bundle of hundred-dollar bills in the other. Kyle moved over to the hatch that led into the cargo hold and looked in, past Oksana, and saw not only the girls sitting on either side of the boat's interior benches, but that the bow of the boat was flush with stacks of cash. Kyle peeked over the top of the boat and saw the wooden crates and got an idea.

*****

Kyle had the go-fast boat at idle speed through the channel avoiding the floating debris of what was left of the collapsed tunnel that ran between the two small islands. Once he was clear, Kyle had the boat pushing its engines near maximin speed over the moonlit waters of the outer banks of the Grand Turks Islands. The navigation system on the boat shows they should have plenty of fuel to make it to the main island and according to the map Kyle just needed to circumvent a few more islands along the way.

Once the boat cleared the protection of the next island the seas became a little rougher as the wind picked up. The hull of the boat began skipping over the choppy water like a flat rock tossed with full force. Out of the corner of his eye, Kyle could see Kamiko's wrapped body flopping on the deck in rhythm with the boat. He looked back over his shoulder and saw Jillian waving one arm to slow down as she held onto Aiko with the other. Kyle immediately pulled back on the throttle.

Kyle quickly checked in with the girls down in the hold. He saw all of the girls were wearing life-vest and holding onto each bracing themselves with their feet up against the two wooden crates which now contain the loose bundles of cash. Oksana gives Kyle the thumbs up then goes to check on Aiko.

Jillian was checking on Aiko's makeshift bandage, "It looks like the duct tape has come loose. You're going to have to slow it down a bit. She's already lost enough blood as it is."

Kyle pulls out a fresh strip of duct tape and adds it to the rest of the metallic triage, "That's going to have to do." Kyle tosses the empty roll behind him. "Has she come too at all?"

"Momentarily, but then she passed out again. We've got to get her help and soon."

247

"According to the navigation we're close."

"Let's hope that's close enough."

Although Kyle was trying to avoid as many other boats along the way, his new plan was to take a more direct line to what appeared to be the largest port on the island. Before long he was in sight of the harbor lights.

As Kyle got closer to the port he could see what looked like a man securing down his seaplane next to a fueling station near the end of the dock. Kyle slipped the go-fast boat up behind the seaplane. As he was tying down the line at the stern of the boat Oksana came out from the storage area.

Kyle knew he needed to hurry as this might be their only chance. "Oksana, go back inside and get the satchel. Put about five bundles of cash in it and bring it to me, fast."

Oksana didn't hesitate. She quickly returned with the satchel and tossed it to Kyle. Kyle motioned to Oksana and Jillian to stay with the boat as he walked over to the pilot of the seaplane. Kyle noticed on the tail of the plane was a logo for West Wind Tours. The pilot saw Kyle heading his way and was already sizing him up.

"What can I do for you?" asked the seasoned pilot.

"I'd like to rent your seaplane."

"Are you a licensed pilot in these parts?"

"I'm afraid not, Sir."

The pilot was ready with his standard reply, "Then you're going to have to rent me, too."

"How much per day?" inquired Kyle.

The pilot could sense a money maker and played it for all it was worth. "How many days?"

"One."

"How many passengers?"

Kyle thought about it. "Six."

The salty pilot had gotten a good vibe from Kyle. He noticed the expensive satchel he was carrying and the intense interest from the woman and the young girl watching from the boat. "How does $1000 sound?"

"Do you have extra storage in the tail?"

"For what? Nothing illegal?"

"I have two crates as well."

"That will be added weight and take more fuel."

Kyle was growing impatient but didn't want to piss off the guy. Kyle took the bartering as a way of just doing business with the locals.

"How about $1500 and we call it good?" Kyle replied.

The pilot thought it over and gave Jillian and Oksana a smile. "Good, it is. We can leave first thing in the morning. How about 8 a.m.?"

"How about I double it if we leave right now?"

Kyle might have overplayed his hand too soon. The pilot twisted the well-chewed toothpick in his mouth then tossed it aside. "How about $5,000?"

Kyle reached into the satchel and handed the man a bundle of twenties. That was a yellow paper trap wrapped around it that read, $10,000.

Kyle hoped the added incentive would work. "That's for no more questions and the added fuel."

"Where are we going?"

"Miami."

The grateful man saw his chance to maybe get another seaplane to expand his tour business and nodded. "Miami, it is."

The pilot went over to a nearby gas pump and began refueling the plane.

Kyle made his way back to the go-fast boat and asked Oksana to have the girls come out of the storage area and for her to get a few more bundles of cash ready. As each girl came up from below, Kyle slit an eight-inch slice in one side of the life vest and slipped in a bundle of twenties. Each girl walked off the boat with $10,000 and

Kyle hoped it would be enough for each of them to start over.

The pilot was curious as he counted seven young women walk past him still wearing their life vests, but he was paid not to ask any more questions and he was trying his best to account for his silence.

Together, Kyle and Oksana carried one of the crates toward the seaplane. The pilot had just finished refueling and opened the back hatch on the tail section to allow the crate to be loaded.

Kyle had other plans. "I'm going to need you to open the door to the back seat and help me load the two crates. We can seatbelt each one into a seat on the far side."

The pilot did as he was asked. Once the crates were in place, Kyle took a quick glance around and saw that the dock at their end was clear. Under the cover of darkness, Jillian helped Kyle bring Yuki's body up to the plane and they loaded it into the tail section while Oksana stayed with Aiko. It took the pilot a minute to register Kyle's request of six passengers with only four seats left on the plane.

He had to break his silence. "Excuse me. Is that…?"

Before he could finish, Kyle replied, "Passenger number five."

While the pilot took the time to pace in a circle weighing the ten large versus passenger's five and six, Kyle and Jillian had already loaded Kamiko's body into the tail section with Yuki's and had the door closed.

The pilot was about to make his point that there might be an ethical problem here. When the pilot saw something in the woman that was helping Kyle load the plane.

"Excuse me. She looks a lot like the First Lady?"

Kyle handed the keys to the go-fast boat over to the pilot. "How is your eyesight now?"

The pilot helped Aiko and Oksana off the boat. He saw that Aiko was injured and had lost a lot of blood.

Kyle reiterated his terms, "We have to go now and no more questions. No one can know we were here."

The pilot nodded and as Kyle helped everyone onto the seaplane, the pilot maneuvered the go-fast boat over into a nearby slip. He grabbed a plastic five-gallon bucket used for bait off the boat moored next to him, filled it with water, and doused the area where Aiko had been sitting to wash away a small pool of blood. He tossed the empty bucket back onto the other boat and scurried back over to the seaplane.

It wasn't long before the seaplane was skipping across the water and lifting off headed north on its six-hundred-mile journey toward Miami.

*****

Pres. Dalton was inside the Oval Office sitting behind his desk looking past the U.S. flag that stood proudly next to the window. Something caught his eye. A loose thread from the yellow trim that bordered the flag. He took the corner of the flag in his hands and started to slowly pull on the damaged thread. He didn't seem to care that the yellow braided decorative trim was unraveling and coming away from the flag. He just continued to slowly pull on the thread. The phone rang, and he didn't bother to answer it. He then realized he had undone 10 inches of the flags trim. There was a knock at the door. Dalton let go of the desecrated flag.

"Come in."

Agent Malone entered. She was carrying an iPad. "Sir, we have movement on both Majestic and Red Butterfly. They seem to be traveling at a high rate of speed over the Caribbean, Sir. Looks like a flight out the Turks islands."

Dalton met Malone in the middle of the room in front of his desk. "Where are they exactly?"

"They just cleared the Caicos Islands with a heading that looks to be possibly Miami International Airport."

Dalton sat back on the edge of his desk.

Agent Malone thought the president was looking a little pale. "Sir, are you alright?"

"Yes, I'll be fine. Can you locate Wintersteen and have him get the First Lady's detail on alert and have my plane standing by?"

"Yes, Sir." Agent Malone took her leave.

"Thank you, Sienna."

As the door shut behind agent Malone, Dalton was clearly frustrated, and the grip he had on the pencil he had been holding became so tight, he snapped it in half.

CHAPTER 44

Fifty miles off the coast of Florida an F-18 fighter jet pulled up parallel on the left side of the seaplane. The pilot didn't have time to think when over the radio he heard, "Pilot, my name is Capt. Levy and my friend to your right is Capt. Harris." Capt. Harris tipped his wings and dropped back. "On the authority of the President, we would like you to maintain your altitude and change your course heading to two-eight-five. We will be landing at Naval Air Station Key West. Do you understand my instructions?"

Before the pilot could answer, Kyle said, "Tell them you understand and will follow his instructions."

The pilot could barely talk. "Should I tell him about the First Lady?"

Jillian leaned forward in her seat. "I think he already knows I'm onboard."

"Yeah, right."

Jillian could see the pilot was understandably nervous. "Not to worry, I will tell him you are responsible for helping to save my life."

The pilot keyed his radio and confirmed his instructions to follow.

Jillian had a request, "Can you ask them to have an ambulance standing by for one of our passengers who's in need of immediate medical treatment? She has a life-threatening wound and has lost a lot of blood."

"What about passengers five and six?"

Kyle replied, "Let's not mention that just yet."

******

The seaplane landed at NAS Key West and was met by an ambulance as it rolled to a stop. As Aiko was being transferred immediately to the ambulance, Kyle grabbed one of the arms of the paramedics and got his full attention.

Jillian and Oksana overhead Kyle tell the paramedic. "She's lost a lot of blood and you need to know, she is pregnant."

The paramedic replied, "We will do our best to save them both."

Oksana wouldn't let go of the gurney as the paramedics rolled Aiko over to the ambulance. The second EMT was using his fingers to feel for a pulse on Aiko's neck as they made their way across the tarmac.

"I can't feel a pulse!"

The EMT went for his stethoscope as the other continued pushing the gurney but was being slowed by Oksana hanging on to the side rail.

The paramedic placed his hand over Oksana's. "You're going to have to let go."

Oksana had never felt such pain before. The pain filled every part of her aching body as Kyle came up behind her and put his hand on her shoulder.

Without turning around, Oksana said, "Tell me she's going to be okay."

The two EMTs lifted Aiko's gurney up into the back of the bus and began working on her vitals. The back doors were open and Oksana, along with Kyle and Jillian were able to watch the team work on Aiko. Oksana didn't quite understand all the words they were using but she knew it wasn't good.

"I got a pulse! It's weak but viable."

"Respirations are shallow. Bagging her."

"The wound is clotted so I'm going to leave the duct tape in place."

"Start an I.V. of 500 milliliters of Ringer's lactate."

The two EMTs continued to work in unison adding fluids and working the manual resuscitator, trying to make Aiko's vitals stable enough to transport.

As one EMT was wrapping the BP cuff around Aiko's arm an alarm sounded.

"Blood pressure's dropping!"

Another alarm sounded.

"I can't find a pulse!"

As one EMT ripped open Aiko's shirt the other applied the defibrillator pads to Aiko's chest and side. "Clear!"

Oksana could see Aiko's body violently arch up off the gurney then fall back down.

"Again!"

"Clear!"

Oksana could feel Kyle's hand trembling as he gripped her shoulder to hold her steady. They all watched as Aiko's body contorted once more and fell motionless.

One of the EMTs checked Aiko's pulse.

"Let's go!"

The second EMT hopped out of the back of the bus, closed the doors, and ran to the driver's side door.

The sound from the doors on the back of the ambulance as they closed sent a shock wave through everyone. Jillian stepped in and took Oksana in her arms as the ambulance rolled Code 3 as it left the tarmac. As the emergency lights dimmed and the siren faded off into the distance, Oksana turned to Kyle, her eyes filled with tears.

Oksana pleaded with Kyle once more, "Please tell me she is going to be okay! Tell me!"

Kyle did his best to comfort Oksana but through her tears, she saw Kyle was fighting back tears of his own.

All Kyle could say as he brushed Oksana's hair back from her face was that he too shared her pain. "I know, I feel it too."

Thirty minutes later, the president's plane landed at the Navel base in Key West. The First Lady's assigned Secret Service agents, Weller and Lynch, were making their way down the portable stair platform. By the time they reached the bottom Jillian was there waiting for them. The men couldn't believe it was the First Lady. Although she was a little battered and bruised, they had never seen her looking so forceful and in charge.

"Ma'am are you alright?" asked Weller.

Agent Hague noticed the First Lady's clothes were literally falling off of her and were exposing her breasts. Hague took off his jacket and wrapped it around her shoulders.

"Thank you."

"Ma'am, we are under orders to get you back to Washington as soon as possible."

"Gentleman, we're not leaving just yet."

The First Lady began to walk over to where Kyle and Oksana were waiting with the pilot of the seaplane who was being detained by airport police. The Secret Service agents followed without question.

As the First Lady approached the police officer, agents Weller and Lynch flashed their credentials.

Jillian was in no mood. "Why is this man in handcuffs?"

The airport security officer was still a bit awed that he was talking to the First Lady. "Ma'am, we noticed he has two crates in his plane with no shipping labels of any kind and he refuses to open the back storage on his plane."

Before he could go any further, the First Lady set him straight, "Those crates are coming with us and the contents he is protecting happens to be two fallen members of my security team and their gear."

Agents Weller and Lynch looked at each other out of the corner of their eyes and out of loyalty, played along. Weller used his baritone voice with authority, "The President of the United States has sent us down here to retrieve our fallen agents and you would be doing service to our country by releasing them to our custody. We will get them back to their families as a soon as possible. I'm sure you understand."

The security officer was about to reply when Jillian cut him off and pointed to the seaplane pilot. "And as far as this man is concerned, he saved my life and I owe him a debt of gratitude for his service. So, I would appreciate it if you would remove those handcuffs, now!"

The security officer looked back at his partner who had already taken a step back and was letting his partner take the heat. With his anxiety levels going through the roof, the security officer uncuffed the pilot.

Jillian hugged the pilot and whispered a sincere, "Thank you."

The pilot knew it was his time to go while he had the chance. "Thank you."

CHAPTER 45

The President's motorcade was waiting at the private end of the tarmac when his plane returned to Andrew's Airforce Base that morning. Dalton stayed in the protective vehicle until the stairs were in place and the door to the plane opened. One of President Dalton's Secret Service agents opened the car's door and Dalton was able to board Air Force One with little to no fan fair.

Just like at the beginning of the story, Pres. Dalton was in his private office sitting at his desk. A battered and bruised Kyle Morrell was sitting across from him.

This time Dalton's words had a deeper understanding. "It wasn't supposed to turn out like this." Dalton stood and went to the wet bar. "As President, decisions have to be made, and not all outcomes are predictable."

"As President, you disgraced yourself by risking everything including your family. For what? Do you not have any honor?"

Dalton poured himself a drink and went back to his desk. "What does honor have to do with it? There's no honor in politics! Don't you know that by now? Tell me, Kyle, was it worth risking your life for a woman who disgraced her own family and a girl whose father was willing to sell her to the highest bidder?" Dalton took a sip of his drink. "Was it worth it?" Dalton took another sip of his drink waiting for Kyle's answer.

Kyle's answer was from his heart, "She was worth it."

Dalton swirled the ice in his drink that was as cold as his words, "Everything has a cost."

Kyle's silence spoke volumes. Kyle's hands gripped the end of the chair arms so tightly his fingertips were turning white.

There was a knock at the door. Oksana entered, and she too had a few scratches and bruises. She was wearing a new commemorative T-shirt that was one size too big for her that had a large AF-1 logo on it. Her hair was a bit matted and dirty. Kyle stood and started to lead Oksana out the door.

The First Lady, Jillian, approached the office and met them at the door wearing a blue dress. She took Oksana by the hand. "Let me walk you out, Oksana. I want to thank you for everything. You saved my life."

Jillian and Oksana exited the plane.

Dalton reminded Kyle of the cost of doing business. "Kyle, if you had the chance, would you do it all over again knowing what you know now?"

"In a heartbeat."

*****

The First Lady was in her private quarters of the White House, sitting at her desk with her hand over her heart. She took a sip of water and set the glass down near Kamiko's satchel. Jillian removed a burned CD from her computer, placed it in a jewel case, and slipped it into a pre-addressed Manila envelope. She grabbed the second envelope along with a third disc.

The First Lady left her office and handed the two Manila envelopes to one of her Secret Service detail. "Mail these."

Agent Lynch took the envelopes.

The First Lady didn't break stride as she headed toward the Oval Office.

Agent Weller joined the First Lady. He looked over at Jillian and could tell by her bumps and bruises she had been through an ordeal. "May I ask, ma'am. Are you alright?"

Jillian stayed focused on the task at hand. "Never better."

*****

As Jillian walked up to the door of the Oval Office, she walked right past the Chief of Staff before letting herself into the Oval Office. She was followed by agent Weller who stopped just inside the door of the Oval Office. As Jillian entered, Dalton was sitting on the front edge of his desk. Wintersteen and agent Malone were sitting in the settee area.

Jillian kept her cool and her eyes on Dalton. "We need the room."

Wintersteen and Malone started to stand. Dalton put out his palm face down and they stayed seated.

Jillian presented a disc. "You might want them not to see this?"

Dalton called Jillian's bluff. "They have clearance."

Jillian looked at agent Malone then back at Dalton. "Among other things, this disc contains proof there is a sleeper agent within the White House that has a standing order to take you out if anything should happen to Kamiko Masato."

"Who is that?"

"Last night Kamiko was killed in a black op you sanctioned."

"Does your disc show who this person is?"

Jillian didn't answer.

Dalton's wry smile did not go unnoticed. "I didn't think so." Dalton saw in Jillian's eyes she had more to say. Dalton turned to Wintersteen and Malone. "Can we have the room, please?"

Wintersteen and Malone stood and headed toward the door. Wintersteen left first. Agent Malone looked back at Jillian. Before leaving, she paused knowing the First Lady knew her role was more than an executive assistant.

After agent Malone's exit, agent Weller followed and close the door behind him.

"What is it that you want for that disc?" Dalton asked.

"I want you to get my human trafficking project fully funded, so we can locate and rescue every one of the girls that Kamiko has sold on this list."

Dalton was waiting for the other shoe to drop. "Done."

Jillian tossed her husband the disc. "Along with the evidence Kamiko was black mailing you with, that copy is missing one name off the list. The Sleeper. Oh, and I also have the code to activate." Jillian took a moment to let her words sink in, and continued, "I alone have that copy. Kyle has a copy of the disc you're holding and so does my lawyer."

"Welcome to the game."

"This is no game. These are people's lives. So many people have died, good people, and for what?"

CHAPTER 46

Kyle was sitting on the back porch watching Oksana walk along the beach.
Oksana was wearing the necklace she had given to Aiko for her birthday. Kyle finished his Coke and tossed the empty can into the recycling bucket that was on his back porch. Kyle checked his watch. He saw Oksana slowly walking his way. He waved his hand to have her hurry up. Oksana ran up the rest of the way to the house.

Kyle waved Oksana his way. "Time to go."

Inside the beach house, Kyle and Oksana each took a packed suitcase that was sitting inside the front door and headed out.

*****

Kyle was driving with Oksana along the Oregon coast. They were listening to a local radio station. Oksana reached over and turned off the radio.
They both sat there in the quiet for a moment.

Oksana continued to look out the window beyond what was out in front of her. "Are you surprised we were invited to the ceremony? And why did it take over six months to recognize Aiko as a Masato?"

"Although Aiko's father was young, he was also a prominent man. To have a daughter with his sister was more than a scandal. Plus, having both of her parents bringing shame for their actions, also brought dishonor to the family."

"So why now?"

"I was told it had to go to Council and I guess it took them this long to find Aiko's actions were worth honoring, despite what her parents had done."

"But we are not her family."

"I guess we were the closest thing to what she had left."

"I miss her."

"I miss her, too."

CHAPTER 47

A dark sedan was heading down a country road lined with beautiful Japanese Maple trees full of fall colors. The car came to a stop in front of a large, ornate, ceremonial building. The car was greeted by two valets. Each valet opened a back-passenger door and Kyle and Oksana exited the car. Kyle was holding an urn.

A small group of the Masato family members greeted Kyle and Oksana.

"Hello, my name is Hosi Masato. Welcome to Japan."

Kyle acknowledged, "Thank you, Hosi-san for inviting us. It is an honor."

Hosi turned to Oksana. "You must be Oksana. I have heard very nice things about you from my conversations with Kyle-san."

Oksana bowed. "You have a beautiful home and thank you for letting us share this special time with your family."

Hosi returned the bow. "I see what you mean, Kyle-san. I like this little one." Hosi went in for a hug with Oksana.

Oksana was surprised but liked the gesture. Kyle looked off into the distance through a gap in the trees and saw a stone mantel with an urn on it. Kyle handed the urn he carried over to Hosi, who in turn handed to a woman. She accepted the urn, bowed, then took her leave to take it down the path into the ceremonial space and set it on the mantle next to the other urn. Once she was respectfully away, other family members and friends moved in to greet and welcome Kyle and Oksana to Japan.

*****

An elaborate memorial service was in progress in a beautifully designed traditional garden. It reminded Kyle of Portland's Japanese garden but only in its use of bamboo and flowers. This one was different because it had a magic to it. Kyle looked around and saw the outpouring of love that was in progress as the Masato family and friends had gathered for the loss of one of their family. I guess that was it Kyle thought to himself. It had to be the love and care that went into the upkeep of the grounds, its positive energy. The sun's light seemed to bring a happiness to everything it touched.

Incense was burning in a dark brown Japanese cast iron bowl between the two urns. It wasn't fancy, and Kyle liked that about it. All he could think about was that it must have been in the family a very long time and how many funerals it must have been used for. Looking around Kyle didn't feel sad. It was the energy of the garden and how the family felt about life and not losing someone but celebrating their journey. Each urn now had a picture in front of it, one with an older picture of Kamiko in front of it from when she was last at the Masato home and the other with a picture of Aiko. Kyle had taken the picture of Aiko at the coast. It was one of the few that he actually caught her smiling. Oksana had picked it out because she had heard Kyle once tell Aiko it was his favorite.

Kyle was in a suit and Oksana had been dressed in a traditional Japanese kimono. They felt honored as they were allowed to sit with the Masato family. A Shinto priest began chanting a Sutra. Kyle felt Oksana lean her head on his shoulder. He also noticed a few of the guests had seen this tender moment between them. When Kyle and the guests made eye contact, he was a bit surprised to see them smile. He took it as a good sign that he and Oksana were accepted.

After the service, Hosi took Oksana's hand and asked her and Kyle to follow him.

*****

A dojo had been transformed into a beautiful ceremonial room. As they entered, everyone removed their shoes. Hosi gestured for Kyle and Oksana to kneel and sit on one side of a low table and he would take the other.

Hosi smiled and took a deep relaxing breath. "First of all, I would like to thank you Kyle-san for honoring our request to send our Kamiko home to us. Also, for

271

acceptance to our invitation to lay them both to rest. I know this must bring up very strong feelings for you and Oksana as it does for our family."

Kyle respectfully nodded. "The honor is ours."

"I can only begin to understand all you have been through and all you did to try to keep Aiko safe. May your journey going forward be a new beginning."

Hosi turned his attention to Oksana. "Speaking of family, that is why I have brought you here to this room. I have something I would like to present to you Oksana."

Oksana looked at Kyle in disbelief.

Hosi removed a silk that had been covering a katana on the table in front of them. The katana was the most beautiful sword Oksana and Kyle had ever seen. There was one diamond on the handle just below the hilt.

Hosi slipped on a pair of white gloves then picked up the sword. He rolled the one of a kind katana slightly to let the light shimmer off its scabbard. "This was to go to Aiko for bringing back honor to our family. I believe she would be honored if you, Oksana, would accept it in her name."

Kyle shifted his elbow into Oksana prodding her out of her daze.

Oksana changed her focus from the sword to Hosi. "Are you sure?"

"Yes, I am sure." Hosi had more to share, "Let me show you something special about the katana." Hosi pointed out the single inlaid diamond in the top of the handle, just below the hilt. "This diamond here was made from some of the ashes of Aiko's father, Ichiro." Hosi turned the katana over and showed a second diamond on the other side. "This diamond was made from her mother Kamiko's ashes."

Oksana thought such a priceless item needed to stay within the Masato home. "I can't accept this. I am not family."

"This is why you should. You honor our traditions and our family has already discussed this. It is what we all want."

Oksana turned to Kyle to get his reaction and she saw for the first time, there were about 20 family members standing behind them. Oksana turned back to Hosi who had slid the katana back into its scabbard and held it out to Oksana.

"Kyle-son, thank you again for trusting in the Masato family. We know all that you have done and sacrificed to protect your family and we will honor all of your requests in Aiko's name."

*****

Oksana was walking down the dock past a series of houseboats. She had the katana in a special soft pouch strapped over her back. She followed Kyle to the same houseboat Kyle had taken Aiko to for refuge when they first met.

They passed a sign on one of the houseboats that read, FOR SALE. Contact Alicia at Davenport Real Estate, Portland.

Kyle stopped at the unit with its faded strands of small lights in the shape of icicles that were attached the edge of the roof. The porch light was on. Kyle slipped the key into the lock.

*****

Oksana entered the warm house. The fire place was going strong. Oksana removed the katana from the pouch. She handed the katana to Kyle. He, in turn, held out the katana in front of him. "I have something of yours."

The light from the fireplace was casting a bold shadow of a silhouette onto the wall. Another shadow appeared to extend from that shadow. A set of hands held up a new born baby.

Aiko's said, "And I have something of yours." Aiko presented Kyle with his child that he was meeting for the first time. "Your own Shadow Warrior."

Made in the USA
Columbia, SC
09 August 2019